SHADOWS IN THE SNOW

SHADOWS IN THE STARS
BOOK 2

T.W.M. ASHFORD

Copyright © 2024 by T.W.M. Ashford
All rights reserved.

No part of this book may be reproduced in any form or by any electronic or mechanical means, including information storage and retrieval systems, without written permission from the author, except for the use of brief quotations in a book review.

Any characters in this publication are fictitious and any resemblance to real persons, living or dead, is purely coincidental.

Cover design by Tom Ashford

DARK STAR PANORAMA

Dark Star Panorama is the shared universe of sci-fi stories in which *Shadows in the Stars* takes place. Other series include *Final Dawn, Kapamentis Crime* and *War for New Terra*.

To hear about new releases and receive exclusive free content, sign up for T.W.M. Ashford's mailing list at the website below.

www.twmashford.com

BOOKS IN THE "DARK STAR PANORAMA" UNIVERSE

Final Dawn Series

- The Final Dawn
- Thief of Stars
- A Dark Horizon
- The New World
- The Tin Soldiers
- Ghost of the Father
- The Stellar Abyss
- The Edge of Night
- The Fatal Dark

War for New Terra Series

- Sigma
- Iron Nest
- Royal Blood

Shadows in the Stars Series

- Shadows in the Stars
- Shadows in the Snow
- Shadows in the Stone

Kapamentis Crime Series

- A Cut Below
- Cut to the Bone
- Cut and Shut

- The Final Cut

Standalone Novels

- Saturnalia

SELECT NON-DSP TITLES

- Checking Out (Box Set)
- Blackwater (Box Set)
- The Portrait Lingers Like a Whisper
- Gerald Oddman

SHADOWS IN THE SNOW

CHAPTER ONE

The storm ravaging the city planet of Kapamentis howled like it were wounded from the ships piercing its obsidian clouds. A crooked spear of yellow-white lightning streaked through the perma-night sky between sluggish frigates and racing speeders and struck the pylon of a mile-high skyscraper. Giant holographic Oortilian girls, slender and blue, danced between the neighbouring towers.

Sheni squatted on the slick ledge of a luxury apartment building's eighty-seventh floor as rain lashed against its tinted windows. He squinted across at Gecki, who was fumbling about in the pouch hanging around her neck. This plan was reckless, even for them.

"How do we know they aren't in?" he yelled across at his reptilian crew mate.

"What?" she shouted back.

"I said..." Sheni shook his head and pointed to the black glass. "They could be looking out at us right now!"

"Nah." Gecki found what she was looking for – a small, black and red puck with a laser tip embedded in its underside. "The owner's not even on-world. Hasn't been for a whole two cycles now."

"Doesn't mean there won't be security."

"*Course* there'll be security." Gecki attached the puck to the window between them. "But just the digital kind. Nothing we haven't handled before."

With the flick of a tiny switch, the puck travelled in a circular motion across the window pane. A red glow spilled out from underneath. Sheni could barely hear the hiss of laser cutting through glass above the sizzle and slosh of rain.

He tightened his grip on the girder to his left and forced himself to not look down. If he slipped, he wouldn't splatter against the garbage-strewn streets for the best part of a minute. Plenty of time to regret his life decisions leading up to that messy moment.

The laser-cutter finished its lap and deactivated. Gecki wrapped her claws around the puck and pushed inwards. The circle of glass slid out with ease and made a dull thud as it hit the floor. Too robust to shatter. If an alarm got tripped, it was silent.

"Wait here," she rasped before slipping through.

Sheni did as instructed. His clothes were soaked through, glued to his skin. Kapamentis was cold, especially almost a hundred storeys up, and the fierce wind was doing nothing to keep hypothermia at bay. Despite his reservations about breaking into such a swanky apartment, he desperately wanted to get inside, away from the storm.

Gecki reappeared in the opening a minute later, transforming from a mere shimmering, hazy outline to her regular mint-green self. As a Eureptix, she could shift the colour and pattern of her scales to match her surroundings. It was a little unsettling at first, and the effect sometimes made Sheni's eyes water, but it sure proved handy in their line of work.

"The primary intruder alarm's offline," she said, waving a black market data drive at him. "Get inside, quick."

Sheni inched along the narrow cornice, his heart hammering, terrified he was going to slip and tumble to his death, and carefully clambered through the hole. The cut glass looked smooth to the touch, but he didn't fancy testing it. He emerged into a living space doused in soft, warm light by lamps that resembled wind chimes. The walls and floor were panels of pale brown wood trimmed with darker mahogany. The climate-controlled air smelled of sandalwood. Furniture resembling a semi-circular ottoman occupied a conversation pit set into the middle of the living room floor. Inside the walls were glass cases and cabinets, deliberately minimalist, each shelf containing only one or two display items. A transparent staircase to his left led up to the floor above. Sheni assumed that's where they'd find the bedrooms. He spotted a dining table just past the staircase, through a wide, doorless archway, and beyond that a pristinely clean kitchen area. The front door to the apartment stood at the end of a short corridor directly ahead of him.

He lingered by the window, rainwater pooling around his boots.

"What's wrong?" Gecki asked, peeling back her lips to reveal rows of sharp, yellowing teeth.

"I've just got a bad feeling about this gig, you know?"

"Hey. You're the one who said he only wanted to steal from people who don't deserve what they've got. And stars, I'm fine with that. Means the stuff we take's worth more. But it also means better security. Rich people can afford to *stay* rich. So quit complaining and keep an eye out for tripwires."

Sheni reluctantly followed her into the apartment. It was fine, he told himself. Everything worked out all right in the end. The place was deserted; the alarms deactivated. A good haul from this place would keep them in the black for a standard cycle or more.

So why, given his track record of good luck, did something gnaw away at his gut like a rat trapped under a hot bucket?

A security box was over by the front door, its plastic panel left hanging open. That was how Gecki had disabled the alarm system, he guessed. He was surprised she hadn't just ripped it off the wall with her claws.

Sheni was distracted from his growing concern by the various artefacts on display. An ancient book of scripture, its pages brown with age and burnt at the corners. An unsheathed sword with a ruby-red grip. The skull of a sabre-toothed beast, long extinct. Patheer, the collector to whom the apartment belonged, had impeccable taste. Any one of these items would fetch a high price from Peggi Slim, the fence at the Corpse & Casket.

"Should I grab any of this stuff?" he asked.

"Nah, leave it. Unless we strike out, then pocket whatever you can. It's just the idol we're after."

"Patheer is gonna know someone broke in, right? The hole in the window's a dead giveaway."

"Sure, sure." Gecki scratched her chin. "But the less we take, the less incentive our rich friend here has to send somebody after us. This is just one apartment. Patheer has loads. Chances are she won't even realise what's missing."

"Crooks like Patheer operate on principle, Gecki. She'll

know. Especially when she takes a look at the camera footage."

"What, those things?" She jabbed a claw at the small black eye nestled in the corner of the ceiling. "Switched them off at the same time as the alarms."

"I'm thinking of the exterior cameras belonging to the property manager. You know, the ones that'll show Xotl dropping us off in the *Silver Hart?*"

Gecki paused in thought.

"We'll wipe the tower's servers when we're done," she rasped. "Same data drive I used here should do the trick."

"If you're sure," Sheni sighed. "It's both our funerals if you're wrong…"

"Go check upstairs, will you? My contact told me the idol's kept in some kind of safe. Like a mini vault. Shout if you find something."

"What if the neighbours hear?"

"In *this* apartment?" Gecki snorted. "We could set off a bomb in this place and the other residents wouldn't hear a thing. Hurry up and look."

Sheni stomped up the see-through staircase. It was built with transparent metal – aluminium, probably – rather than glass. He could tell from the way each footstep sounded dull. Plus, way too easy to scratch otherwise. He'd been right to assume the bedrooms were upstairs. There were only two, though. A spare for guests was tucked away at the end of the landing. The rest of the second storey was dedicated to the host.

He checked the spare bedroom first. Despite being fairly modest compared to the rest of the apartment, it was still nicer than anywhere Sheni reckoned he'd stayed in his life (which admittedly only amounted to a series of hovels on an increasingly inhospitable Earth, the jail cell of an Ark ship, and the cargo hold of the *Silver Hart*). It contained a nest of cushions and feathers in place of a bed, though he imagined it was just as comfortable, if not more. A couple of wooden chests stood against the wall. They weren't locked, but they contained nothing interesting – just spare sheets and glow-orbs.

It hardly seemed likely Patheer would hide anything super valuable somewhere guests might accidentally find it, so Sheni mentally crossed the spare bedroom off his list.

Back to the main bedroom. Another, much bigger nest-bed. Man, Sheni would have loved to get some proper sleep in one of those things. His hammock back on the ship always left him with a stiff neck. Ignoring it, and hoping the occupant wasn't so paranoid that she slept directly on top of her safe, Sheni checked inside the antique cabinets and stands and behind the fancy portraits. There were no holo-screens in the apartment, he noticed. No projected artwork. Everything Patheer owned was tangible, tactile. It was a privileged approach to interior design most citizens of the galaxy could never hope to replicate.

No word from Gecki yet, just the scratchy sound of priceless vases being shoved around downstairs. He tried the en-suite, and though the bathroom was nothing like a human toilet or shower – he suspected Patheer cleaned herself by rubbing her furry body on the mossy roots creeping out from the frothy jungle vines, but honestly it was anyone's guess – he was fairly confident there was no secret safe in there, either. Gecki was welcome to double-check if she didn't trust his judgement.

That just left the walk-in wardrobe. Two rows of rotating plinths contained dozens of tailored suits and flamboyant social robes. He spun them, pushed them aside in the hope a safe was hidden amongst them somewhere, but no such luck.

He pulled at the mirror, but no matter how hard he strained, it wouldn't budge. Then he leaned against it in frustration and heard a click. As he stepped away again, the right-hand side of the frame popped open an inch.

"I've found something," he shouted down. "Get up here."

As he waited for Gecki to join him, Sheni let his gaze fall on the view from the bedroom. Though the windows were mirrored for anyone trying to view the apartment from outside, residents could see out with perfect clarity. Hundreds of ships sped across the city skyline, weaving around steam vents and chimney stacks. The round neon hull of a monstrous low-orbit resort moon broke through the storm clouds. None of the passing traffic seemed to have noticed the glaring hole in the window just yet, despite the light surely leaking out. Or perhaps they had, and the Ministerium was already on its way. But they probably didn't care. People on Kapamentis had too many problems of their own to worry about.

"Is it the idol?" Gecki asked, bursting into the bedroom behind him.

"I haven't checked yet," Sheni replied, shrugging. "But I can't imagine this place has too many secret rooms."

"You're an expert on clandestine architecture, are you?" she snarled, stomping past him. "Gods, I have to do everything myself..."

He followed her back into the walk-in wardrobe. She curled a claw around the edge of the mirror and opened it cautiously. A reinforced safe door, as suspected. Gecki plugged her black market data drive into a slot on its front, ran a program to disengage the electronic locks, and then pushed the door open. There was another room on the other side, but it couldn't have measured more than two by two metres. There was no overhead light fixture. The floor was black tile, the walls and shelves draped in similarly dusky cloth. A few documents and data drives lined the shelves, but Sheni barely noticed them. The only object of note was the small, gold statuette sitting on the backlit plinth in the centre of the room.

"There it is," Gecki said, licking the saliva from her teeth. "The Charakhan Idol. Pure gold. Only one in existence, apparently. Their civilisation died out millennia before any species in the Ministry left their planet for the stars. It was reported as stolen from the Orpik Gallery of Galactic History about six cycles ago. I'm guessing that was Patheer's doing. Or her supplier's."

"Shouldn't we, you know, return it to them?"

"Ah, the Gallery is full of artefacts stolen from countless empires." She winked at Sheni. "They're no angels. If they want it back, they can bid for it in the auction like everyone else."

Sheni watched in silent awe as Gecki turned the idol over in her hands. It was such a small thing, really. Like a tiny sarcophagus, modelled on the exaggerated features of a long extinct species. What wonders it must have seen over the millennia, excavated from ancient dirt, passed from the hands of one spacefaring civilisation to another, until one day ending up in the dark cupboard of some dodgy antique collector's wardrobe.

The rat in his belly kept on gnawing.

"Gecki, I've been wondering about something..."

She rolled her yellow eye. The milky one stayed in place.

"Yes, Sheni...?"

"Why were the lights already on when we came in?"

Gecki suddenly stopped inspecting the statue. Sheni felt what remained of his confidence ebb away.

"We should be leaving," she said testily, pocketing the idol and retrieving her comm-link from the pouch around her neck. "Xotl, we need extraction right away. Hello? Xotl, are you there?"

Gecki shook the device, checked its tiny screen.

"Can't connect with the *Silver Hart*," she snarled in barely-contained panic. "This godsdamn apartment must be blocking the signal somehow."

"I guess we're leaving via the front door then, coz I ain't waving Xotl down from that ledge. So much for sneaking out unseen."

They left the bedroom and hurried down the transparent staircase. Rain continued to spill through the hole Gecki cut in the window. They spun round and headed towards the door of the apartment, then suddenly stopped short.

Patheer and her two burly bodyguards blocked their escape.

"Now, where do you think *you're* going?" she purred.

CHAPTER TWO

Sheni and Gecki sat beside one another on the spongey sofa in the conversation pit, but nobody was doing a lot of talking. The golden Charakhan Idol had been placed on the squat coffee table in front of them. The pair of bodyguards stood above the pit with their arms crossed. From the walls watched the taxidermy heads of numerous dangerous beasts. Soothing handpan music played quietly in the background. Patheer prowled back and forth between them, debating what to do with the two intruders.

At least Sheni hadn't been forced onto his knees. If he *was* to be executed, this was much more comfortable.

"Took you long enough to find this thing," Patheer said, as much to herself as to Sheni and Gecki. "So I assume none of my competitors sent you. Not even Regulus Slake is *that* amateur."

Patheer was a member of the Felis Vestris species. Though they had a representative on the Ministerium of Cultured Planets' council, and Sheni had even enjoyed a pleasant game of cards with one of their kind at the Corpse & Casket once, they weren't exactly known for their assimilation into the wider galactic community. They tended to view themselves as superior to their interstellar neighbours, which explained why Patheer's bodyguards were also Felisian. Bipedal and commonly reaching seven foot, they had the cold, glossy eyes of an apex predator and were covered with thick fur from head to toe. Their ears were large and pointed, often adding yet another foot to their already intimidating height, and three-inch prehensile claws lay hidden within their enormous paws. Patheer's fur was a silky purple-black colour, but Felisians came in a great variety of shades and patterns. Her bodyguards were ginger-brown and grey-white respectively. Despite their outward prejudices, there was surprisingly little discrimination within their own species, though this was possibly a result of their terrible colourblindness. As far as they were concerned, even the lowliest Felisian outranked everyone else... especially those, like Gecki, who didn't even have the decency to be a *mammal.*

Patheer and her bodyguards had been watching them scramble about looking for the secret storage compartment ever since the *Silver Hart* dropped them off outside the apartment window. With those big ears of hers, Patheer probably heard them coming even through the sound-proofed glass. The three Felisians had retreated to a panic room hidden behind a display cabinet near the front door of the apartment, just in case. Gecki had snarled at Sheni in an *I told you so* manner when they heard about the second secret room, but Sheni had returned the favour, elbowing her in the ribs when they realised she hadn't *actually* shut down any of the cameras.

"Nobody sent us," Gecki finally replied to Patheer. "We

just heard a rumour that the Charakhan Idol was in your possession and thought we'd try our luck."

"Who gave you that intel?"

"Like I'm gonna tell you that."

Patheer stalked across the sunken lounge area and extended the five long claws of her right paw. She brandished them an inch from Sheni's face. Sheni felt sweat trickle down into the small of his back as he gave Gecki a desperate glance out the corner of his eye. The big cat smelled of musky earth, biscuits and, strangely, cinnamon.

"Okay, fine," Gecki rasped. "It was Dunn over at the Shooting Star. He's always running his mouth about this kinda thing. Said you'd abandoned this place cycles back. That it basically fell under salvage law... so to speak."

Sheni relaxed slightly. Selling out a fellow spacer left a bad taste in his mouth, but it was a damn better flavour than his own blood.

"Salvage? It's my home, you degenerate. One of them, anyway." Patheer retracted her claws and turned to her bodyguards. "Find out who this Dunn person is and how they learned what's in my apartment. Someone needs to shut them up, permanently."

The white and grey haired bodyguard growled obediently and left the room to conduct an extranet search. Patheer turned back to Sheni and Gecki with a sinister smile spreading hungrily across her furry face.

"Now, what to do with you two?"

"Do with us?" Sheni shook his head rapidly. "No need to do anything with *us*. We haven't taken anything, you know? No harm, no foul. We'll, erm, get out of your hair. That is to say," he hurriedly amended, "we'll just be going..."

"Oh, you're certainly free to leave." Patheer gestured to

the hole in the window. "But you'll be going out the same way you came in."

"Ah, yes. The window." Sheni looked at Gecki. "A little bit of harm, then."

"We can pay for that," Gecki said, which wasn't the remotest bit true. As always, the crew was totally skint.

"Pay for it," Patheer said, smiling with a mouth full of white incisors and canines, "you most certainly will..."

Sheni scrunched his eyes shut, expecting his face to slide off his skull like wafer thin ham at any moment. He nervously opened them again a few seconds later when his anatomy remained distinctly un-lacerated.

"But then I'd be out of a good window *and* stuck with a rug cleaning bill," Patheer continued, studying her claws as she curled them in and out. "Neither of which comes cheap. Blood's a pain to get out, especially from a" – Patheer sneered in disgust – "*reptile*. I really don't like it when other people leave me out of pocket. That is rather *their* problem, wouldn't you agree?"

Sheni and Gecki nodded, the reptile with notably less enthusiasm.

"Are you usually better at this sort of thing? Stealing valuables, I mean. As you may have noticed, I'm something of a collector of antiquities."

Sheni opened his mouth, then quickly shut it again. Answering truthfully probably wasn't the best idea if he wanted to leave this apartment with his organs on the inside. They weren't *terrible* thieves. Terrible thieves tended to die off pretty sharpish. But there was a reason the crew of the *Silver Hart* was always broke. Half their gigs ended without any loot.

"Did you ever hear about the Great Hogg-Oth heist?" he asked.

Patheer shook her head. Gecki hissed out a sigh. Here he went again...

"The Chiboraan Eggstraction?" Sheni continued, sweating desperately. "What about the robbery of San Queet the Frivolous?"

"I remember that," the remaining bodyguard growled. "Few years back. Stupid primate lost a pair of antique Drygg statues. Never understood what all the fuss was about, but everyone seemed pretty flustered about it at the time."

"See? We're practically famous." Sheni tried to smile but it came off more like a grimace. "You definitely don't want to whack us now."

Gecki rolled her eyes and snarled in exasperation.

"We were the ones who took out the pirate captains Copperhead and Thunderskull," she rasped at Patheer. "We fought in the Battle for Kapamentis, too. So either tell us which job you want us to pull for you, or slit our throats and be done with it."

Patheer grinned and purred deeply.

"You cold-blooded types are so curt. So primal. But I suppose you aren't without your uses. These past few years since the battle you mentioned have been... *turbulent*. For everyone. Profits are down. You might say that some of my investments have crashed and burned. But perhaps, when presented with the right opportunity, that cunning savagery of yours could be put to better use..."

Sheni cleared his throat. "Excuse me, if I may—"

"*Quiet.*"

Patheer flexed her claws and kept her shiny yellow eyes on the Eureptix dirtying her otherwise pristine furniture. Sheni gulped hard as she weighed her options. Then she waved her paw dismissively.

"No, forget it. As if I would have a job for *you*, lizard."

She scoffed. Sheni's heart fell. "Clearly you're incompetent, and I don't associate with petty thieves any more than I enjoy conversing with you lesser species. But I do enjoy a good hunt. How long has it been?" she asked her bodyguard. "Four years? Five? I invoke the Prowler's Rite."

Gecki groaned.

"Erm, the what now?" Sheni asked.

"In Felisian culture," Patheer explained, "an offended party can demand retribution through a hunt to the death – the Prowler's Rite. For a week the prey may run, hide, prepare themselves however they see fit. Once that time is up, however, they're fair game. *Literally* game," she added, glancing at the taxidermy heads nailed to the wall above them. "The tradition is still legal in Ministerial space under" – she clicked her claws together twice in thought – "cultural protections, is it not?"

The bodyguard shrugged. "There's a loophole."

"Hold on a minute," Sheni spluttered. "This doesn't need to get out of hand, you know? There has to be another way we can make this up to you."

"Of course!" Patheer purred convivially. "You can always pay to have the mark lifted. Makes the hunt more interesting for us both. But the levy must be in proportion to the slight…"

Gecki flashed a worried look at Sheni as Patheer performed some quick mental calculations.

"The cost of a replacement window, compensation for emotional distress…. Yes, I think one hundred thousand credits should suffice."

"A hundred thousand?" Gecki snarled. "That's insane! It's not like we got away with the idol!"

"One hundred thousand credits *each*," Patheer continued. "Bring me that, and the mark is lifted. I'll forget this little transgression ever took place. Fail to produce, and my associate and I will take what you owe in blood."

Her bodyguard narrowed his feline eyes.

"What if we can only get half that much?" Sheni asked, avoiding eye contact. He doubted he could source even five percent of the desired amount, let alone fifty.

"Then perhaps my associate will only kill half of you," Patheer replied. "You should hope it's a half you don't often use."

"Any chance of setting up a payment plan?" Gecki rasped sarcastically.

"You have a week."

"Be reasonable, lady." Sheni spread his arms out wide. "You know there's no way of getting that many credits in that short a timeframe."

Patheer darted forward, hooked a claw under Sheni's chin, and tilted his head up to face her own.

"Oh, I'm counting on it," she purred. "Your time starts now."

CHAPTER
THREE

Parking charges were extortionate on Kapamentis, so while Sheni and Gecki unsuccessfully infiltrated Patheer's apartment, Xotl had kept the *Silver Hart* in a low energy hover beside a CyberSplice Inc. logo around the back of a nearby skyscraper. Now they were back in orbit, their engines switched off, while dozens of private cruisers and supply shuttles shot past their cockpit windows.

"We are so freakin' screwed," Gecki snarled, pacing back and forth. "Patheer's gonna kill us for sure."

"Two hundred thousand credits," Xotl muttered to themself. "My, that is a lot."

"Come on, guys." Sheni tried to remain positive. "We've stolen stuff worth that much before. More, even!"

"No, we haven't," Gecki snapped. "We *owed* Copperhead more than that when we failed to deliver the goods we promised."

"Oh yeah..."

"Well, how did we get out of that debt in the end?" Xotl

asked eagerly. Since the Xocha never left the ship, they sometimes missed out on the finer details of heists.

"We kidnapped a crew of galactic heroes so Copperhead could stick them in his prison barge." Embarrassed, Sheni scratched the back of his neck. Not their finest moment. "And it still wasn't enough to get out from under his thumb. Real psychopath, that Copperhead. We, erm, had to kill him in the end. Blew up the barge, too. But we rescued those heroes first!"

Gecki bared her teeth in fury.

"Curse Patheer and that godsdamn idol. I should have ripped that stupid *malkin's* head off when I had the chance!"

Sheni and Xotl exchanged a look. Well, Sheni thought they did. It was hard to tell exactly where the alien starfish was looking, given they had minute eyes all over their five arms and around their central beak. But their arms were bent curiously, Sheni was sure of it. They were both thinking the same thing. Unfortunately, and despite Sheni frantically shaking his head behind Gecki's back, Xotl elected to ask their reptilian captain the question playing on both their minds.

"You're not going through The Change, are you?"

Sheni winced.

"How old do you think I am?" she roared. "I've got decades before that happens!"

"My apologies, Gecki," Xotl spluttered. "My understanding of Eureptix physiology is amateur at best..."

She growled again, and Xotl hurriedly gyrated back to their pilot's seat with a series of arhythmic slapping movements. 'The Change', as Xotl put it, was an inevitable part of the Eureptix lifecycle. Gecki had been born male, and had morphed to female a few cycles after reaching sexual maturity. When she was no longer capable of producing eggs, she'd switch back to male again. It was a perfectly natural process, one Gecki didn't need to be ashamed of even amongst a multi-species crew, but that didn't stop it from being a sore point.

"Let's all take a second to chill, all right?" Sheni patted the air for calm. "We can figure this out if we put our minds together. Where's Alan, anyway?"

He glanced to his left and almost had a heart attack. Alan was suddenly standing on top of the computer terminal next to him, the two bulging eyes that occupied the majority of his small, spherical body staring in opposite directions to each other, his spindly arms and legs sticking out like bent dandelion stalks caught in a breeze. He was dribbling from the corner of his thin, perpetually smiling mouth.

"You really think *his* mind is going to contribute much?" Gecki snarled.

"That's rude, Gecki." Sheni patted Alan on his gormless green head. "You should apologise."

Gecki went to lash out at everyone again, then finally softened and collapsed into her chair.

"Sorry, Alan," she grumbled.

"Okay, let's think about this," Sheni said once everyone had taken a seat. "How much would that Charakhan Idol have got us?"

Gecki bobbed her scaly head from side to side.

"Maybe as much as a quarter of a million credits," she rasped. "Minus Peggi Slim's fencing fee, of course."

Sheni whistled. No wonder Gecki had been so eager to follow up on Dunn's rumour. That kind of take was worth the extra heat, even for someone as typically risk-averse as Gecki.

"So we just need to find another idol," he said. "Not the

same thing, obviously. I know it's unique. But something equally rare and valuable, you know?"

Gecki laughed.

"You think artefacts like that are just lying about?"

"No, but... like... Kapamentis is full of rich knobs, isn't it? Who knows how many priceless relics they've got stashed away!"

"What do you want to do, cut holes in random penthouse windows until we find something? You're an idiot. Patheer was *supposed* to be in another system. We never would have gone near her place otherwise. If we go breaking into apartments without researching the owners first, someone's gonna shoot us."

"Yeah, I guess you're right. Dammit." Sheni clicked his fingers together. "What about that museum you mentioned, the Orpik Gallery of Galactic History? If they used to have the idol, they must have loads more valuable stuff. And they're basically thieves themselves, right? We wouldn't have to feel bad about taking anything."

"I wouldn't feel bad anyway. You're the one who refuses to steal from anyone who doesn't deserve it. If we'd stuck to robbing the poor, we wouldn't be in this mess."

"Gecki..."

She growled irritably and shook her head.

"Gallery's a no-go. *Way* too much security for us to handle."

"Can't you sneak past it? You know, camouflage yourself?"

"Changing my scales to match the colour of the walls won't stop me from interrupting their laser grids, nor will it get me past the retinal scans. I'd trigger every alarm in the institute within ten seconds of slipping inside. We'd need a lot of expensive tech to break into a place like that."

"And we have barely a credit to our name," Xotl reminded them. "Enough for food and fuel, but no more."

"Impecunious," Alan gurgled.

"Well, I'm all out of suggestions." Sheni shrugged. "*You* come up with something, Gecki. It was your idea to listen to that drunken fool at the Shooting Star in the first place."

"You were up for it, too!" she spat, leaning across the aisle. "Least you were till you realised how high up her window was."

"Exactly. It's normally *your* job to talk *me* out of bad ideas, not the other way around!"

"Can we not argue, please?" Xotl's arms wilted. "Bickering won't get us any closer to finding those two hundred thousand credits."

Sheni ran his hands through his hair.

"Why do we always get ourselves into these messes?" he groaned.

Gecki scratched at the flaky scales underneath her chin. Her shedding was getting worse. Sheni wondered if it was due to stress, or whether both her testiness and flakiness were tied to The Change after all. Of course, she could just be moulting...

"I might have something," she said cautiously. "Maybe. Do you remember me telling you about the *Lucky Quark*?"

"I think so..." Sheni furrowed his brow. "Wasn't that the fancy casino ship that crashed a few years back?"

"That's the one. And when it went down, it did so with millions of credit chips on board. Normally, the digital share of that balance would be automatically wired off-ship in such an emergency. Standard protocol. Gotta keep the shareholders happy, right? But whether the planet's storms blocked the signal, or the ship's transmitter got wrecked in the crash, that transfer never took place. All those credits are just sitting there. An immense physical and digital reserve."

"Yes," Xotl replied, "and I remember why we didn't go chasing after that score when you first brought it up. It's the same reason nobody else has retrieved those credits already. The climate on Gressil Prime is too dangerous. The *Lucky Quark* casino cannot be reached."

"Until now," Gecki said, tapping a key at her terminal with her claw. The same images on her screen appeared on Sheni's computer and Xotl's dashboard. They showed a satellite view of shifting cloud patterns.

"You're right, Xotl," she continued. "Gressil Prime is plagued by violent storms, some of which last for centuries. Only a few pockets of the planet are habitable, and even those aren't anyone's idea of easy-living. The *Lucky Quark* crashed in an area known as the Gellar Valley. The weather there is especially bad. Winds that can strip a ship of its shielding. Snow so cold, just touching it can leave your fingers black with frostbite. Nobody who's tried to drive or fly their way through has ever made it back."

"You're really selling this," Sheni said.

"The Gellar Valley storm follows a regular pattern. Has done for more than seven hundred cycles. Roughly fifteen years and three months while the storm is practically impenetrable, followed by a period of reduced intensity lasting four and a half days. The last time a lull was measured was almost fifteen years and three months ago to the rotation. If we're quick, if we leave *right now*, I reckon we can get to that vault."

"Says who?" Sheni snorted. "No offence, but forgive me if I don't trust the opinion of some crackpot on the extranet. And you're not exactly a meteorologist, you know?"

"I don't need you to trust me." Gecki jabbed a claw at

her screen. "I need you to trust the Kilonova Corp. That's the company behind the *Lucky Quark*. It's their shareholders' credits I want to steal. And they're sending a private strike force to reclaim the cash this week. They announced it in their quarterly report."

"I'm sorry, you want the four of us to go up against *mercenaries?*"

"No, I want us to empty the *Quark's* account and be gone before the corpo-mercs even get there."

"The data looks legitimate," Xotl spluttered, "and every job carries a certain degree of risk. But this is far too dangerous, Gecki. I don't know what's come over you recently."

Gecki threw back her head and hissed.

"I don't think you two understand. If we get inside the *Lucky Quark's* vault, we won't just have the two hundred thousand credits we need to pay off Patheer and get her mark lifted from our heads. We'll each be multi-millionaires. Richer than in our wildest dreams. We'll never need to pull a job for anyone ever again."

"Big risk," Sheni mused, chewing the nail of his index finger. "Big reward."

"The *biggest* reward."

"It's suicide if you're wrong."

"And it's murder if we spend the next week trying to scrape together the credits we need. Face it, guys. We could pull off the best heist we've ever done, *and* sell the *Silver Hart*, and we *still* wouldn't have nearly enough money to call off Patheer's hunt. We signed our death warrants, breaking into her penthouse. She'll kill us if we don't cough up."

"She'll only kill you two," Xotl pointed out.

"Oh, as if Patheer wouldn't bump you and Alan off for the fun of it," Gecki snarled. "I've told you what I think. It's the best gig we've got. I know I'm the captain, but I say we vote on it. Limbs up if you want to take part in the heist of a lifetime."

She raised a scaly claw in the air and fixed Sheni with an expectant glare. For a few seconds he simply sat there, filling his cheeks and then blowing out slowly. Then he clapped his hands together and broke into an acquiescent smile.

"Screw it," he said, much to Gecki's satisfaction. "I'd rather die doing something big and crazy than at the paws of a feline supremacist. I'm in."

Xotl went to great pains to lower all five of their arms, which gave the impression they were melting backwards over the cupped sides of their egg-chair. Everyone turned to face Alan, the deciding vote. He was still standing on the same computer terminal as before, smiling and dribbling in a world of his own, his favourite red-handled wrench raised valiantly above his head.

"That shouldn't count," Xotl insisted. "He was doing that already."

"Three votes to one." Gecki shrugged triumphantly. "Looks like we're heading to Gressil Prime."

"I suppose it's no chitin off my suckers," the Xocha said, spinning around to type the planet's coordinates into the dashboard. "You're the ones who'll have to leave the safety of the ship."

"Yeah, about that." Sheni leaned forward and squinted at his reptilian crew mate. "When you said 'reduced intensity' before, just how reduced did you mean?"

Gecki reclined in her seat as the *Silver Hart* skipped into subspace. She suddenly seemed incredibly engrossed in an article on her data pad.

"I guess we'll see, won't we?"

CHAPTER
FOUR

Sheni had been taking a nap in his hammock down in the cargo hold when Xotl's disembodied voice burst through the ship-wide comm speakers, telling everyone to get up to the cockpit. Five standard hours after leaving Kapamentis's orbit, they were finally in the Gressil star system.

He joined Gecki and Alan around Xotl's egg-chair.

"Ladies, gentlemen and unidentified green nuisances of the *Silver Hart*," the starfish said, reluctantly clicking switches across the dashboard as they prepared to leave subspace. "I give you... Gressil Prime."

The stars popped into place as their ship skipped back into the regular set of dimensions. One star was far bigger than the rest – a white dwarf that glowed dimly, its nuclear fusion a bitter memory. Gressil. Four planets and a thick belt of iron-rich asteroids orbited the aged stellar remnant. The largest of those astronomical bodies, Gressil Prime, now loomed before the *Silver Hart*. Twice the size of Earth, it was almost marble in appearance. Hurricanes and storm clouds the size of continents blanketed the entire world, snow-smothered mountains and frozen oceans alike, in swirls of greys and white.

"Oh, the place doesn't look too bad," Sheni said in a bid to inject a little optimism into the room. "Just a bit chilly, that's all."

"Just a bit chilly." Xotl laughed, which consisted of a series of clacking noises. "My species cannot even walk upon the planet's surface. Putting aside the risk of infection, temperatures that low would suffocate us in an instant. I hope you packed your thermals, Sheni."

"Thermals?" He followed Gecki back down the cockpit. "How cold are we talking, Gecki? I normally just throw on a jacket."

"Jacket won't cut it," she replied distractedly. "Temperature fluctuates from one region to the next, but even in the settlements it rarely climbs above minus thirty degrees centigrade."

"Minus thirty? You said *minus* thirty, right? That's like Arctic weather!"

"I'm guessing that's a cold place for you humans?" Gecki shrugged. "The Gellar Valley will be much worse. You'll need to wear your enviro-suit. I will be. Us reptilians are especially susceptible to the tundra."

Sheni groaned. He hated the suit. It was clunky and uncomfortable. They couldn't afford a better model even when they weren't in mountains of debt, but he supposed he should be grateful it wasn't patched together with strips of duct tape. Gecki's enviro-suit had improved padding and climate control, but it was still a great many years old, a relic from back when she captained a one-lizard crew. They'd even bought Xotl a rubbery, mostly transparent outfit a few months back so the starfish could join the rest of the team on safer expeditions and trips to the Corpse & Casket. Xotl had accepted the suit in an uncharacteristically emotional display of gratitude, but they hadn't even tried it on.

Ah well. A wedgie from a poor-fitting spacesuit was better than freezing to death.

"Tentacles up," Xotl said from the pilot's seat. "It looks like we're not alone."

A jet-black frigate came into view as the *Silver Hart* drifted towards the planet. Narrow and trapezoid in shape. Sleek and stylised. Corporate, not military. A red company logo was painted down its flank.

Kilonova.

"Damn the gods," Gecki snarled. "Well, we know why *they're* here. I was hoping we'd get the jump on them."

"You might still have the chance. I cannot be certain, but it doesn't look as if they've deployed any drop ships yet. They're probably still analysing the storm patterns."

Gecki growled impatiently. Alan quietly slipped out the cockpit door.

"We need to get down to Gressil Prime, *now*. They're gonna be using way better tech than us, and it'll be hard enough getting ahead of them as it is. How close can you get us to the Valley, Xotl?"

"Not close at all," Xotl replied in alarm. "I can't get within a hundred miles of that crashed ship, and you know it."

"Don't be such a coward. We'll never get ahead of that recovery team if we don't take some godsdamn risks!"

"Even during a comparatively quiet spell, the Gellar Valley storm will rip the *Silver Hart* down to its component pieces. It's not a question of cowardice, Gecki. The Kilonova Corporation isn't sending its ships in there, and its *their* credits on the line. If it were possible, it would have already been done, and in far sturdier ships than this."

"Hold on," said Sheni. "If we can't fly to the *Lucky Quark*, what are we supposed to do? Walk there on foot?"

"Ground vehicles," Xotl explained. "That's how most locals get from one outpost to another. Staying clear of the Death Zones, of course. The closest settlement to Gellar Valley is Borel-Six. I'm certain you'll be able to hire a rover from there."

"With what credits?" Gecki rasped.

"We're not entirely penniless, and you'd be surprised how far credits will stretch on a backwater planet like this. Considering the potential payoff, you'd be wise to think of this as an investment."

Gecki turned wearily to Sheni, who shrugged.

"I mean, this job was always gonna be all or nothing, right? However much we pay for a rover, it's not going to make a dent in the two hundred thousand credits Patheer wants in exchange for calling off her hunt."

"Nor will you need those credits after her cronies have drained your bodies of blood," Xotl added. "If you think about it, it's Alan and I who'll be worse off financially."

"Oh, yes." Sheni nodded sarcastically. "Definitely worse off."

"Just get us down to this Borel-Six place as quickly as you can," Gecki ordered. "Stars above. We haven't even breached the exosphere and already the plan is falling apart."

"Better the plan than the ship," Xotl muttered.

The ship began shaking like a wet dog as soon as it hit the atmosphere. Sheni quickly came around to Xotl's reasoning, and, not that she'd ever admit it, the look on Gecki's face told Sheni she was converted, too. Their NavMap route was pre-plotted to avoid the worst of the planet's weather, but the trip down was still rough enough to shake kidney stones loose. Sheni thought he heard the bolts that held the cockpit together rattle in their drill holes.

Then the initial layer of dense cloud cover gave way, and the violent rocking actually got *worse*. Sheni clambered to the rear of the cockpit and strapped himself into his seat. His teeth felt like they were going to tumble out of his head. Through the cockpit windows he watched the grey skyline transform into a whirling black maelstrom. Hail the size of golf balls clattered against the ship's hull. It was a small miracle Xotl could keep the *Silver Hart* from being blown into a tailspin, it was fighting the wind so hard.

But the further they descended, the more the turbulence subsided, and, after a short while, Sheni rose hesitantly from his chair. Outside, fork lightning crackled over mountain ranges cast in twilight purple shadow.

"It's actually kind of beautiful," he mumbled. "You know, in a bowel-emptying sort of way."

"Yes, well, you see one frozen wasteland, you've seen them all." Gecki pulled Sheni into the corridor outside. "Suit up. We need to be ready to move out the moment we land."

They retrieved the various pieces of their enviro-suits from the nearby closet and carried them down into the cargo hold. Sheni got a whiff of stale body odour from the trousers as he bent over to pull them on. Good grief. How long had it been since he wore these last? Not as long as it had been since he got them dry cleaned, that was for sure. Wearing these trousers probably amounted to genocide, the number of microbial colonies he'd be destroying.

His heavy boots smelled even worse, but that stopped being an issue once they were secured to the trousers. Then his hard upper torso, which Gecki helped lock together with the lower half. Then arms, then gloves. He picked up his helmet but kept it under his arm for the time being. There was no need to complete this particular puzzle until he absolutely had to.

Sheni jumped when he realised Alan was standing in the entryway behind him. The tiny green gobstopper had been consumed by a small, brown down jacket, and a woolly bobble-hat was squeezed over his head. The only parts of Alan still visible were his two massive eyes and a pair of spindly bare legs sticking out from underneath his coat.

"I can't believe I'm saying this, given I'm normally the one in Alan's corner... but are you sure you want to bring him along on *this* job?"

"For once, absolutely," Gecki replied, securing her suit's gloves. "Who knows what state the *Lucky Quark* is in. The transmitter might be wrecked, but that doesn't mean the security doors aren't in lockdown. We might need someone to squeeze through some pretty tight spaces. Or blow a hole in the wall, knowing him."

"Okay, but won't he, you know, freeze to death out there?"

"Alan?" Gecki shook her head. "Nah. Weirdo's got a freezing point lower than rum. Saw him get trapped in a nitrogen cooler once. When they finally got the lid off, he was sitting quite happily in a nest of empty nugget wrappers."

Sheni looked back down at Alan, who blinked twice.

"I will never understand you," he said blankly.

The ship shook again, this time with sufficient violence to knock the assorted keepsakes off Sheni's steamer trunk. He thought about putting things back where they belonged, then decided it wasn't worth the bother. They'd only fall back off again.

Sure enough, the ship settled with a lurching crunch.

"I believe," a flustered Xotl said through the ship's speakers, "that we have landed. However bad you expect the weather to be, I recommend you brace for something worse."

The interior airlock door hissed open. Alan tottered inside. Sheni twisted his helmet on until it clicked, then nudged Gecki with his elbow.

"You know," he said, "if we pull this off, we'll be legends."

"Nah." Gecki smirked. "If we do this right, Kilonova won't even know we were here."

CHAPTER FIVE

The exterior airlock doors opened not on a storm, but an aerial onslaught. An impenetrable wall of ice and snow churning in every direction at once. The screech was deafening. The hull trembled. Hailstones smashed to pieces against the doorframe.

Sheni didn't even want to stick out his hand to test how bad it was. He was afraid it might turn to ice and shatter.

"How the hell are we supposed to walk through this?"

"Xotl, you there?" Gecki tested the comm unit in her helmet. "How far is the settlement from here?"

"One hundred and thirteen metres to the south-west," Xotl replied. Sheni could hear their voice through his own helmet, too.

"A hundred metres away and we can't even see it," he muttered in disbelief. "Those habitats might as well be ten miles off. The second we step out of this airlock, we'll be lost. We won't even be able to see the ship!"

"Just follow the compass, you idiot," Gecki growled.

"My enviro-suit doesn't have a compass! It barely has airtight seals! And how's that supposed to help Alan? The poor guy can't even get his eyes to go in the right direction, let alone the rest of him."

Alan stood in the rear corner, swallowed by his thick coat and hat with his arms stuck out at stiff angles, looking like a laundry basket left to spoil for so long that it's sprouted legs and run off in search of a better life.

"He'll have to make do. We're already behind, Sheni. We need to hurry."

"Wait. I have an idea."

He opened one of the compartments hidden in the wall of the airlock. Inside were spools of tethering cable designed for emergencies, should somebody accidentally drift away from the ship while in space. Sheni found a pair of shorter cables intended for orbital repair work and unclipped both. He used one to link his suit to Gecki's, and then the other to link his suit to Alan, which involved tying the cable around the little guy's waist as tight as humanely possible.

"You lead the way," he said to Gecki, "and we'll follow."

"Actually not a bad idea for once," she rasped, impressed. "Just don't lose those cables when we're done with them. All right." She bared her teeth. "Here goes nothing…"

Gecki marched into the tempest. Sheni lost sight of her within seconds. He gritted his teeth and stomped after her before the cable lost its slack. He hoped Alan had the sense to keep close.

"Hold on tight, Alan!" he yelled over his shoulder.

It was like walking under a particularly vehement waterfall, only one that blasted him from either side as well as downward. Thank goodness his enviro-suit didn't come equipped with haptic feedback, because it was getting battered worse than a keyring in a washing machine. Something hard – a clump of ice, probably – smacked into his visor, and for a second he was terrified it had cracked. Luckily, even a cheap helmet like his was made of sturdy stuff. He couldn't keep up with Gecki, though. The cable grew taut and he was tugged rudely forward through the dense snow.

A dark shape flurried past his head. Then once more, back the other way. Sheni spun around in terror. Something was stalking them through the storm, circling in for the kill.

Then he heard the giggles carried eerily on the wind.

"Alan?" he cried out. "Is that you?"

A green bowling ball stuffed into a puffy jacket slowly glided past his face, dangling on the end of his tether like a kite in a hurricane. Sheni hurriedly reeled the cable in, all the while still being tugged forward by a relentless (and totally oblivious) Gecki. Thank the stars he was wearing gloves, because otherwise his hands would have been torn to ribbons.

"Don't let go, buddy! I've got you!"

The view was the same wherever he turned. No habitation modules, no *Silver Hart*, and certainly no mountains in the distance. Just dark, whirling grey winds and the detritus they threw about like weapons. All he could do was follow the cable connecting him to Gecki and hope she was leading them in the right direction.

Then he saw it – a warm, red glow deep amongst the monotonous madness. A beacon set up to indicate a perimeter or an entrance of some kind. They had to be getting close to the settlement. Either that or it was a lighthouse, warning them away from the edge of a deadly cliff.

The cable tethering him to Gecki grew slack. Sheni tried to swallow but his throat was too dry. He hoped this meant she'd reached safety, and not that something terrifying had swept down to snap the cable and carry Gecki off to its nest. He reeled Alan further in just in case.

"Will you hurry up, human?" Gecki's voice crackled over their private comm channel. "I'm freezing my scales off over here!"

Sheni breathed a sigh of relief and forced himself to push on through the sludge. Her dark silhouette gradually loomed through the gloomy snowfall; she was standing beside a heavy-duty door inside a shallow alcove set in the side of a curved metal shelter. He barged his way into the alcove next to her, then gave the cable a good, hard yank. Alan came tumbling in behind them.

Against all odds, his bobble hat remained on his head.

"How do we get inside?" Sheni shouted over the howling wind.

"I don't know," she snarled back. "I've tried the comm panel beside the door, but no-one's answering. Maybe the place is deserted. Easy for a place as stranded as this to get wiped out..."

"What about this thing?"

Sheni pointed at the wheel-crank in the door, half submerged in snow. Gecki grabbed it with both of her clawed hands and tugged it counter-clockwise. It turned freely, offering no resistance, and the hatch swung outwards.

"An unlocked door," she said with a shrug, "is as good as an invitation."

"I don't care what's in there," Sheni yelled. Even with the suit on, his teeth were chattering. "I'm not standing out here a moment longer."

The three of them pushed past one another through the gap. Inside was a small chamber of exposed metal leading to another industrial hatch. A barrier designed to keep the heat in and the bad weather out. Realising the second door wouldn't open until the first was closed, and eager to put all memory of the storm behind him, Sheni heaved against the handle and sealed them inside.

All was suddenly, hauntingly quiet.

"Let's meet the locals," Gecki said, spinning the other wheel crank as Sheni unclipped everyone's cables. "Or what's left of them, anyway…"

The door opened, a waft of warm air smelling of motor oil and reed smoke puffed past them…

…and everything was pretty normal, actually.

Crates and grain sacks were piled up by the inside of the door like supplies at a dock. Fluorescent light strips dangled from the exposed beams on the ceiling. Loops of wire hung from the walls. A grey-skinned Drygg – an intelligent species of horned beetle rarely seen not wearing its distinctive bulky power armour – looked up at them from his stock checklist and nodded in curt acknowledgement. Clearly, Sheni thought to himself, the locals weren't surprised by visitors.

"I guess this outpost isn't quite as remote as we thought," he whispered to Gecki as they strolled past a muscular Alpha Rhoden loading plastic barrels onto a forklift.

"Yes," Gecki replied cautiously. "If Borel-Six has been overrun by an alien parasite, it's certainly a benign one."

The outpost reminded Sheni of the Corpse & Casket space station. Barebones, no frills. People constantly working to keep their little part of it from falling to pieces, in turn ensuring the outpost as a whole didn't rupture and kill everyone inside. Power units rumbled, climate-controlled atmospheric generators hissed and dripped. Each cramped room and pre-fabricated corridor bolted onto the last like a sprawling table of domino tiles. All of the signposted directions pointing to lab rooms, storage modules and residential quarters were painted either on spare scraps of sheet metal or the rare panels lining the walls themselves.

Not that Gecki was soaking in any of the scenery. She had her snout buried in her data pad.

"You on the extranet?" Sheni asked.

"Yeah, hooked up to the station's relay. Signal's terrible, though. Says here Borel-Six started as a research facility studying anomalous weather events. Twenty-something scientists. Then families got brought over, people who wanted to start again somewhere remote. Now it has a population of almost five hundred and fifty. Proper little town."

Sheni couldn't imagine travelling light years across the galaxy just to pitch up sticks in a snowed-in dump like this. But then again, he slept in the cargo hold of a stolen ship. Who was he to judge?

"Hey, new faces." A gangly Garnidian took a break from inspecting a leaking pipe in the ceiling to approach them. "Can I help you with something?"

"Yeah, we were hoping to rent a rover," Sheni replied. "You got a garage or anything?"

"Sure do. You'll want to speak to Drairy. She's the mechanic round here." He gestured straight ahead down the hallway, then to the right. "Just follow the concourse clockwise from here. I'm not sure what she has in her bays right now, mind you, coz Grott and Filch are out on a survey run. Course, you're always welcome to grab a drink at Marcy's while you wait."

They looked through the open doorway to their left. A Drygg bartender rinsed out a pitcher behind her counter while two locals sat solemnly at the same table, not speaking to one another, in an otherwise empty break room. Old holo-posters on the walls reminded residents of the importance of safety equipment and radiation checks. Weird glockenspiel music tinkled out of a small speaker hanging by its cable in the corner of the ceiling.

Sheni raised his eyebrows at Gecki.

"I mean, I *could* do with something to warm me up, you know?"

"No time." Gecki shoved Sheni forward and smiled amicably at the Garnidian. "Thanks for the help."

They followed the engineer's directions, only having to backtrack to keep Alan from wandering off once, passing through curved, trembling tunnels connecting the sporadic modules of the ever-evolving outpost. Sheni spotted a med clinic, a cheap motel for visiting traders (he reckoned he'd prefer to sleep in his ship, but maybe once inside, nobody wanted to brace the storm again), and a security station. Then, after ducking through yet another tunnel quaking from the fury of the snowstorm, they arrived at Drairy's garage.

Not that there was any kind of sign or emblem to signify who owned the place. Just an off-world road sign nailed to the wall, a giant rubber tyre propped up beside an ill-fitting door of scrap metal, and a lot of clanging and cursing leaking out from inside. Sheni shrugged at Gecki and entered.

"Be with ya in just a moment," somebody with a chasmic voice shouted as a bell jingled above Sheni's head.

It was a garage, all right. Engines and driveshafts hanging from chains suspended from the rafters. Dark stains tarnishing the concrete floor. More tyres piled up into leaning towers of rubber. The intoxicating odour of petroleum and engine grease. And what looked like somebody's modded cruiser up on a ten-foot jack, its underside removed and its skip drive exposed. A thumping trollish tune blasted out from a jukebox somewhere, but it could barely be heard over the screech of an angle grinder.

The screeching stopped a few seconds later and a burly Alpha Rhoden stomped out from behind a shelf of spare parts, wiping her elephantine hands clean of oil and gunk with a threadbare rag. She was big, even by her leathery species' standards. Her horn had grown a full four inches from her snout.

"Name's Drairy," she grunted. "What can I do for ya?"

"Carburettor," Alan said, waddling off toward a large bin of miscellaneous ship components.

"You need a carburettor?" Drairy asked. "Got loads of 'em. Just tell me your model and I'll hook something up."

"Oh, no, don't mind him," Sheni replied. Not that he knew what a carburettor was. Put on the spot, he would have said it was a special kind of Italian pasta. "Idiot just says whatever he sees. We were actually hoping you could loan us a rover, if you've got one."

"Yeah, I've got something sitting in the back, if you're interested." Drairy beckoned them over as she headed toward the ginormous set of industrial doors at the back of her garage. "Better bring your friend, too."

Alan hopped out of the bin and waddled after them. He caught up just as Drairy was threading her arms through a heavy duty overcoat.

"Gets pretty chilly in the lot," she said, catching their curious expressions. "All right, step through. And be quick about it."

She punched a button beside the doors and they grumbled open along their rollers. Drairy ushered everyone through before the doors were even halfway open, and then she activated another button on the other side to quickly lock them shut again.

"There ya go," she said, shivering. "Only set of wheels I've got at the outpost right now. But ain't she a beaut?"

Sitting in a much sparser, frostbitten section of garage was a large and extremely dented six-wheel rover. 'She' was facing another giant set of doors, big enough to drive through, and Sheni realised they were now standing in another, much larger barrier chamber just like the one they passed through to first get inside the outpost, only for vehicles rather than people. It made sense. How could Drairy work on anyone's rides otherwise?

He didn't know how Drairy could stand how cold it was. Already he could feel the frost creeping through the flaws in his enviro-suit. Alpha Rhoden hides were super thick, he supposed.

"She's something, all right," Gecki rasped, inspecting the rover. "These wheels good for all terrain?"

"Wouldn't last very long on Gressil Prime if they weren't," Drairy grunted jovially. "Most people favour tracks for the weight displacement, but she'll cut through the snow just fine."

"And the chassis," Gecki said, pointing to all the dents running along the rover's side. "Looks like it can take a beating."

"Yeah, it's... Sorry, what do you need this for?"

Gecki and Sheni shared a tiny, worried glance.

"We were thinking we'd take a drive out toward Borel-Five," Sheni quickly replied. "Explore some of the landscape on the way. We just want to make sure we won't run into any trouble if we stray into, you know, *inadvisable* territory."

"Borel-Five?" Drairy huffed through her large nostrils. "That's a long way to take the rover. D'ya mean Borel-Four?"

"Yeah, that's what he meant," Gecki snarled. "Stupid human's always getting his outposts mixed up."

The Alpha Rhoden squinted her beady eyes and studied the two of them curiously. At some point Alan had climbed onto the roof of the rover, and was presently twanging its comm antenna like it were the string of a double bass.

"You two ain't thinking of driving out to the Valley, are ya?"

"What?" Sheni snorted. "No. Course not. That would be insane, wouldn't it?"

"Yeah, it would." Drairy tilted her head down in an aggressive stance. "Doesn't stop morons from thinking they can drive out to that crashed ship, though. Last time a chancer took one of my rovers out east, I never got it back."

"Look, we're not gonna go that way, all right?" Gecki snarled impatiently. "We just need a rover. We'll pay you credits to borrow it. What else is there to talk about?"

"I don't *have* to loan my rovers to anyone," Drairy replied, growing testy. "Certainly not a pair of off-worlders who don't know their Snagmore Glacier from their Highbottom Trench."

"Woah, woah. Hold on." Sheni stepped in between the two alpha species. "Gecki, go make sure Alan doesn't break anything, will you?"

He turned to Drairy as Gecki slinked away, growling to herself.

"I'm sorry about her," he said in a voice barely louder than a whisper. "She's been quite difficult lately. I suspect she's going through The Change."

The Alpha Rhoden looked over Sheni's shoulder and

visibly softened, like she was maybe prepared to just impale her horn through the reptile's leg instead of her throat.

"I'm just a dumb human. As if *I'm* gonna know the difference between Borel-Four and Five. My species is new to the galaxy. I don't even know which system I'm in half the time. But this trip's important to her, you know? So, what do you say? How much to rent the rover for a day or two? Three, tops."

Drairy grumbled to herself.

"Three hundred credits," she eventually replied. "For *two* days. End of that time, you either drop the rover off here with me or with Krank over at Borel-Four. We've got an arrangement."

Sheni rummaged through the compartment of his enviro-suit where he kept the crew's credits. He counted out the loose coins. This was meant to be spent on food and fuel.

"I've only got two-sixty-five," he said, offering her a meek smile.

"Then at the end of those two days, you bring her back here to me," Drairy grunted, scooping up all of Sheni's credits. "I hope ya didn't plan on visiting long."

She unhooked a rectangular bronze key from her belt and handed it to Sheni.

"Stick that in her ignition and she's good to go. Give me the nod and I'll get that gate open for ya."

Sheni walked over to the rover as casually as he could, flashing a quick thumbs-up to Gecki low by his hip so Drairy couldn't see. Gecki smiled mischievously. Not such a stupid human after all, eh?

He tossed the key to her. She looked down at it in bemusement.

"What do you want me to do with it?" She tossed it back. "I can't drive this thing."

"Are you kidding me?" Sheni hissed. "You used to fly your own ships, didn't you?"

"Yeah, course. But flying a ship's way different to driving something with tracks or wheels! It's weird and two-dimensional. You've used ground vehicles before, yeah?"

"I mean..." He thought back to his life on Earth, before he snuck on board one of the Ark ships shepherding humanity to the stars. "Sure, I drove a truck once or twice, but..."

"You'll be a natural." Gecki patted him on the shoulder before stalking around to the door on the other side of the rover's cabin. "It's Go and Stop, right? How hard can it be?"

"Too hard for you, apparently," he muttered.

"What was that?"

"Nothing..."

Sheni opened the door and pulled himself up into the driver's seat using the overhead handles. The cabin was quite spacious, with two seats up front and room for a good deal of cargo in the back. The passenger door opened, and Gecki tossed Alan into the rear of the vehicle before climbing in herself.

"You good?" she rasped.

Sheni studied the dashboard in front of him. There weren't any pedals for his feet. Just two levers, one which presumably moved the rover forward and backward, and another which turned it left and right. It operated more like a crane than a car, but he reckoned he'd pick it up soon enough. It had been designed with cross-species use in mind.

He took the key, thumbed it into the conspicuous slot in the centre of the dashboard, and gave it a twist. The rover's engine roared into life. Clearly the beast had some power behind it. He guessed it had to, what with needing to hold its own against the storms and all.

Drairy had retreated to a small booth beside the lot's outer doors and was waiting for Sheni's signal. He nodded at her through the rover's window. She opened a plastic case and thumped a mushroom-shaped button. Warning lights on the walls began to flash red. Snow whipped through the gap and peppered the rover's windscreen the second the industrial barriers split apart.

"Okay, I've got the NavMap working," Gecki said, prodding at the touch screen beside the ignition slot. "It should point us to the *Lucky Quark's* last known coordinates without leading us off any cliffs."

With the doors shut and the rover's interior thermometer reading a healthy eighteen degrees Celsius, Sheni unscrewed his helmet and tucked it behind his seat. Gecki did the same. Finally, he could breathe normally again... even if the rover did smell of mildew and mustard.

"Right then," he said, wincing as he nervously guided the rover out of the rapidly freezing lot. "Let's see what this rusty excuse for a moon buggy can do..."

CHAPTER SIX

Driving the rover wasn't too bad. The twin stick system was odd at first, but the longer he spent simultaneously pushing the truck forward and sideways, the more natural it became. It allowed him to pull off some killer drifts, too, not that Gecki was very impressed.

"We're hours behind schedule," was a phrase she'd snapped at him twice already. "Drive faster!" was another favourite.

The rover had been buffeted by crazy winds the moment they left the comparative safety of Drairy's lot, and the weather had only gotten worse the further they drove from the outpost. The vehicle had clearly been designed with Gressil Prime's climate in mind, however, or at least that of another violent planet. Though they could hear the wind crashing into the side of the rover, the cabin barely tilted. And the windscreen must have been heated, because any snow that threatened to enshroud the glass soon turned to slush.

Of course, they hadn't reached Gellar Valley yet. Sheni

tightened his grip on the levers and swallowed hard. These storms were still of the manageable, habitable variety...

"Hello, Xotl? I'm calling from our rover. Can you still hear us?"

Gecki kept trying to reach out to the *Silver Hart*, but the storms were making it hard to establish a decent connection. It would only get worse the further east they pushed. Right now they could tune into the local Borel-Six broadcast channel and not much else.

"I can only just hear you," Xotl finally responded, their voice coming out of the speakers all cracked and garbled. "I am pleased you have acquired ground transportation. I will endeavour to monitor the Kilonova Corporation's activity as best I..."

The signal became too crackly with static, and Gecki was forced to cut comms.

"Looks like we're on our own from here," she rasped.

"Hey, look on the bright side." Sheni glanced across the cabin. "At least it sounds like Kilonova hasn't sent down any ground forces yet."

"Yes," she snarled, "but when they do, they'll be in trucks much faster than this hunk o' junk..."

"I'm pushing it as fast as I can, Gecki."

This wasn't strictly true. He left out the second part of that sentence, which was "without sending us crashing into a ravine." All things considered, travelling fifty-five miles per hour in a blinding snowstorm seemed pretty nippy to him.

Especially given they were trusting the on-board navigation system to have an up-to-date map of the planet's terrain. And though Borel-Six might have started life as a research station, Sheni didn't trust the tech on Gressil Prime to be up-to-date about *anything*, let alone the topography of a region *nobody was supposed to go into.*

The rover's six wide, titanium-spoked wheels ploughed through the dense eiderdown of snow blanketing the barely visible landscape. Its huge, metal, non-pneumatic tyres bounced over larger rocks, rocking on its springy suspension as it landed, and simply crushed anything smaller beneath their twelve tonne weight. If the world outside the windows didn't consist of churning grey nothingness, then it was made of spotless white or icy blue.

Alan remained in the storage area at the back, sometimes sitting on one of the fold-down seats lining the side walls, at other times opening up permanent-looking panels at random and inspecting the wires and motherboards beneath. Nothing important had shut off as a result of his meddling so far, but there was still plenty of time.

Gecki kept tapping her claws against the dashboard and snarling to herself. Sheni wished they could put on a bit of music to lighten the mood.

"Anybody know any good jokes?" he asked.

"You concentrate on the driving," Gecki snapped, "and I'll be in charge of the conversation."

"But you're not saying anything."

"Exactly. *Drive.*"

Sheni gritted his teeth and continued following the NavMap's suggested route, oblivious to whether he was crossing open plains, skimming across frozen lakes or chugging along narrow roads inches from mile-high cliffs. And it remained this way for another two hours, with only the occasional comment from Gecki such as "Mind that rock" or "You're not going fast enough" to break the silence. He contributed a "That was a close one" when they almost crashed into a sheer monolith of translucent ice, but it didn't elicit much of a response from his reptilian companion except a throaty grunt of frustration.

"Are you *sure* there's nothing you want to talk about?" he asked, desperate to stave off boredom, if only for a few minutes. "Something's been bothering you, I can tell. Now's a great time to spill it."

"I'm fine," she rasped, rolling her yellow eye. "I want to get to this vault, that's all. I'll be all smiles once we... Hey, stop!"

Sheni pulled the acceleration lever back hard, then returned it to a neutral position before it could send the rover in reverse. They skidded to a halt a few feet away from the steep summit of a massive snow dune. The snow flurry had cleared with hardly any warning. Sheni had been too focused on getting Gecki to open up to notice.

"There it is," Gecki said, her scaly lips parting in awe. "The Gellar Valley storm."

It wasn't any less terrifying up close than it had been coming down from orbit. A charcoal vortex spitting out lightning and exploding in flashes of scarlet flame. Its fury seemed to push other snowstorms outwards, creating a brief gulley of uneasy calmness. The top of the gargantuan cyclone billowed outwards as it fought against the stratosphere.

"Erm, it doesn't look like it's in a lull to me. How bad was the storm to begin with?" Sheni chewed his bottom lip. "I dunno, Gecki. Are you sure about this?"

"Trust the science," Gecki rasped, brandishing her data pad. "Trust Kilonova's greed."

"Big risk, big reward," he reminded himself. "Okay. What's the NavMap saying?"

"Straight ahead from here." Gecki shrugged. "Down the slope and right into the hurricane. Course, the map's only showing us the ideal route. It doesn't have any data on the weather."

"So as far as the map's concerned, it's a calm and peaceful summer afternoon. Perfect. You know what? I'll keep telling myself the same thing."

He jammed the accelerator forward and let the rover roll down the white hill.

The snow was thicker here, comparatively undisturbed, and it was only as he dropped down into that calmer gulley, protected further from the winds by the mountains rising to either side of the slope, that Sheni realised quite how noisy the ceaseless barrage had been up until that moment. Despite the heavy snowfall, the rover felt as if it were gliding down toward the black hurricane not on wheels but sled runners.

He was tempted to apply the brakes, to pull back on the lever and slow them down to a less breakneck pace, but he feared that once he stopped, he wouldn't have the guts to get the rover moving again.

The smoke-grey maelstrom engulfed the entire windscreen. It became impossible to tell how close to the edge of the storm they were by sight alone.

"Eighty metres," Gecki rasped, glancing down at the NavMap screen. "Fifty metres…"

"I knew this was a bad idea," Sheni said, fighting to keep his eyes open as he gritted his teeth and clutched the controls so hard his hands cramped.

When Gecki gripped the dashboard with her claws hard enough to leave grooves in the plastic, that's when Sheni knew they really were in trouble.

It was like driving into a brick wall. Sheni lurched forward in his seat, kept from crashing through the windscreen only by the straps he'd been sensible enough to secure over his chest. Behind him, Alan ricocheted off the rover's walls like an elastic pinball. The chassis creaked and groaned like a submarine on the verge of collapse. He felt the levers twist away from him, the six wheels of the rover turning and sliding from the sheer force of the winds crashing into their flanks, until he hadn't any idea which direction they were headed anymore.

Sheni desperately wished he hadn't removed his helmet, but there was no retrieving it now. Not that he had that much control over the rover, mind. He could probably go sit in the back with Alan for all the impact he was having on it.

"Where am I going?" he screamed at Gecki, trying to wrench the levers into a neutral position.

"Keep heading forward," she snarled back. The NavMap screen swam left and right like a confused compass.

"Which way is forward?"

The map swivelled three hundred and sixty degrees, inverted itself, righted itself once more, and then began to flicker like a television on the fritz. Gecki threw her claws up in frustration.

"Whichever way you're going now!"

Something flew through the storm and crashed into the windscreen. It resembled a lump of concrete on a rebar, or maybe a piece of roadside crash barrier bent out of shape, but it was gone too quickly for Sheni to get a decent look at it. A hairline crack appeared where it struck, but the screen held. Another big hit like that, though…

"I think we should turn back," Sheni yelled over the din of ice spraying the rover like machine gun bullets.

"This has to be the worst of it," Gecki shouted. "The hurricane'll be calmer once we break through to the eye."

"That Drairy person told us not to head this way. This rover isn't built to withstand weather like this. I've learned to trust my gut, Gecki, and when even *I'm* not optimistic about our chances, you know we're in trouble!"

"Don't be such a hatchling. If you're too scared to drive, get out of that seat and let me take over!"

Sheni tightened his grip on the control levers and let out a guttural growl that burned his throat. He hopelessly wanted to let go and curl up into a ball in the back until all of this was over. But letting Gecki drive seemed like an even quicker path to certain death. The irritable way she was behaving as of late, she'd push the rover until it was nothing but a driver's seat balanced atop a pair of wheel rims.

Satisfied that Sheni intended to carry on for now, Gecki rapped a knuckle against the NavMap.

"We'll be close to the Valley soon," she rasped encouragingly. "Just keep heading the way you're going. It's all flat round here, but the ravine should shield us from the worst of the winds."

Sheni grumbled to himself but kept them on a trajectory towards the north-east. It did *seem* like the storm was slightly less severe than when he first drove into it, though maybe he was just growing accustomed to the sounds of buckling metal and howling banshees. And through the thick vortex he caught glimpses of snow mounds and icy rock pillars, even if they were quickly obscured by the torrential tempest.

"Hang a right, slightly," Gecki rasped, studying the NavMap screen. "You're veering off-course."

"Tell that to the rover, why don't you?" he replied, yanking the horizontal lever as far as it would go.

"Try easing off the accelerator when you're adjusting course. It'll give you a smaller turning circle."

"The accelerator's the only thing keeping us from being blown backwards!"

"Barotropic scouring," Alan gurgled innocently, as he popped up between their seats.

"Not now, Alan," Sheni snapped. "Can't you see we're—"

"Watch out!" Gecki screamed, pointing across the dashboard.

A tidal wave of snow and rock and whatever else the storm had swept up in its homicidal path slammed into the side of the rover with a leaden *boom*. Sheni lost his grip on the controls and wrapped his arms around his head instead. Gecki headbutted the dashboard. Alan flew away from between the seats – his bobble hat still miraculously secured in place – and bashed into the cargo doors at the rear of the cabin. The entire rover listed to the left, briefly skidding along the ground, and then its right set of wheels lifted into the air. The enormous weight of the cabin quickly pulled the vehicle onto its back.

They came to a crunching stop upside down. The engine died. Sheni slowly pulled his arms away from his eyes. Snow covered most of the windscreen, which luckily hadn't suffered any further damage. As far as his blurry vision could make out, nothing on the outside had gotten in, which suggested the chassis was still intact, too.

"Alan? Gecki? Are you guys okay?"

Gecki groaned in the seat next to him. Blood dripped down from her snout, but she was conscious. Alan waddled along the rover's ceiling and held up a button that had been ripped off his coat in the crash. Sheni sighed.

"Don't worry, buddy. I'm sure we can stitch that back on."

"If we get out of here alive," Gecki snarled. She spat out a globule of blood, which shot past her head and splattered on the top of the windscreen. "I think the door on my side still opens. Not sure how long we'll survive trying to walk the rest of the way, though."

"Really?" Sheni coughed. "Your first thought is still to push on and find the *Lucky Quark* rather than head back to our own ship? Do you have a concussion, or something?"

"Patheer will kill us if we don't come up with the credits." Gecki went limp against the straps of her seat, exhausted. "If we don't go back with the contents of that vault, there's no point in going back at all."

"What? That's not true, Gecki. You know, we can—"

A second surge of tundra collided with the rover. Sheni bashed his head against the side of his seat as everything lurched to the left again. Alan and his unfortunate button vanished into the back of the cabin once more.

The rover settled back onto its hyper-malleable wheels with a creaking wobble. Sheni moaned and shook his aching head clear of its last few remaining brain cells.

"What are you waiting for?" Gecki snarled, shaking him by the shoulder. "Get this thing moving before we're on our backs again!"

Sheni hastily thumbed the ignition key, twisted it until the rover's engine spluttered back to life, then rammed the accelerator lever forward. The wheels churned up snow, wrestled with a lack of grip, and then clumsily chugged the rover out of the crater they'd made.

"You're going the wrong way," Gecki rasped angrily. "Look at the NavMap. *Follow the NavMap!*"

"I don't care about the damn route," Sheni replied. "I just want to get out of this storm before it kills us. Look over there."

He pointed through the swirling blizzard. Fast approaching through the hurled wreckages and turgid slush was a giant ridge, a mix of grey and glacier-blue, and at the base of that ridge was a cave mouth wider than the hangar of any battlecruiser Sheni had seen. Twelve-foot stalactites hung from the entrance. The caverns within looked dark and deep.

"We don't know where it goes," Gecki snarled, consulting her precious NavMap.

"Yeah, we do," Sheni replied as the rover shuddered and groaned. "It goes anywhere but here."

CHAPTER
SEVEN

It wasn't quite silent – the rover's engine grumbled and complained, the exterior panels creaked and popped where fresh dents had been added – but compared to the storm outside, the caverns were as quiet as a cathedral at three in the morning. About as echoey, too. The crunch of pebbles under the rover's huge tyres reverberated endlessly off the high, craggy rock walls.

"There have to be miles of tunnels under the snow and ice," Sheni said, staring at all the subterranean shafts and passages they rumbled past. He felt considerably more at ease now they were out of the cyclone. "I wonder how far it all goes."

"Far enough." Gecki, who up until this point had been snarling and snapping at Sheni for departing the pre-plotted route to seek shelter, now smiled and smacked him triumphantly on the shoulder. "It looks like these cave systems cut right through to the eyewall of the Gellar Valley storm. Keep heading that way. Hopefully there's another cave mouth on the far side."

"Eyewall..." Sheni glanced across at Gecki. "As in, the

super dense ring of thunderstorms that circles the eye of the storm? I thought you said we'd gone through the worst of it!"

"Ah. No." Gecki offered an apologetic grin. "That was just a rain band. Or a snow band, I guess. The eyewall's where the storm gets *really* violent."

"Stars above." He exhaled slowly. "I should turn this rover around, you know."

"Millions of credits, Sheni." She undid her straps and climbed out of her seat. "*Each.* Think of how that'll improve our lives. You could captain your own ship, if you wanted. We could travel the stars in a godsdamn fleet."

Sheni sighed. It *was* pretty tempting. No more stocking the pantries with the cheapest tins of sloppy gunk. Weekends getting drunk in the swankiest Kapamentis nightclubs instead of the smelly Corpse & Casket. Freedom to skip to whichever system he wished without first having to calculate the cost of replenishing their somnium reserves. Hell, maybe he could even buy his way back into humanity's good books, pick out a condo on New Terra.

"The credits aren't worth jack if we don't make it back alive," he replied. "We barely survived the outermost band of the storm, and the eyewall's worse, right? Even if we make it through to the *Lucky Quark* – which nobody's done since it crashed, remember? – we have to roll the dice all over again when we head back to Xotl with our winnings."

The rover lurched violently to the left as it collided with a hidden clump of rocks. Sheni wasn't altogether convinced the wheels were still on straight anymore.

"And I doubt this buggy's gonna last the one trip," he added, "let alone two."

"Quit your worrying." Gecki sat on one of the cabin's fold-down chairs. "These things are built to take a beating.

Any serious damage and we can pay that Drairy woman what we owe out of the take. Won't even make a dent."

Alan had climbed onto a seat and opened a maintenance box on the ceiling of the cabin, and had been rearranging wires ever since they entered the cave – fortunately to no effect.

"Stop that." Gecki pulled Alan away and handed him an unwrapped protein bar. "Here. Eat this."

Alan stuffed the bar under the fluffy collar of his coat and gobbled it down with glee. Gecki kept one for herself and tossed another onto the dashboard for Sheni.

"Thanks," he said, grudgingly ripping open the plastic wrapper with his teeth.

For another twenty minutes they trundled on, the tyres bouncing up and down against the uneven terrain, sloping downwards more often than up. It wasn't exactly thrilling, and the view certainly wasn't compelling after the first minute or so, but right then Sheni would have painted skirting boards or pulled open a copy of James Joyce's *Ulysses* over heading back into that damn storm.

The rover's stark headlights flooded the crooked caverns, transforming black rock to white sculpture. Lamps to the vehicle's rear doused the tunnels behind them in a murderous red glow. They were an angler fish swimming indomitably through the black and oily deep.

Over by one of the cavern's twisted pillars, the shadows flickered slightly, like the inverse of a candle flame refusing to be blown out. Sheni squinted through the gloom but whatever it was – presuming there had been something to begin with, of course – was gone.

"Still can't get through to Xotl," Gecki rasped. "Not with the rover's comm unit *or* my comm link. I was hoping the signal would improve now we've left the storm, but the mountain's just as bad."

"Yeah, a million tonnes of stone will do that." He beckoned Gecki over. "Can you see that over by the pillar, or am I going mad?"

Gecki stood with her hands on either seat and peered out through the windscreen. The slinking shadows danced slowly, then erratically, as their headlights rolled past the pillar in question.

"Just a trick of the light," she said with a shrug.

"Nothing lives down here, does it?"

"On Gressil Prime?" Gecki snorted. "Hardly. Intelligent species have struggled to colonise this planet for centuries. This ain't exactly the sort of spot that attracts native fauna, you get me? Not in the Valley of all places."

"I dunno, Gecki. Tardigrades can survive pretty much anything, you know? Even the vacuum of space."

"Yeah, and if microscopic tardigrades try to attack the rover, I don't think we'll have much to worry about, will we? Stop freaking out. Focus on not hitting those boulders, otherwise *we'll* be the ones calling these caves home."

Sheni cracked his neck to the left and right. He was getting pretty tired of driving the rover now. This was Gecki's grand plan, and a stupidly suicidal one at that, and yet now she wasn't even directing them via the NavMap any longer, he was the one doing all the hard work. He may have been in a hurry to get this heist over and done with, but they'd been on the road for hours. He was going to start nodding off if he didn't stop and stretch his legs.

"Hey, check that out!" Sheni slowed the rover to a crawl. "Must be a lot warmer down here than up on the surface."

The rover's headlights twinkled against a small waterfall

trickling out from the rock. Gecki returned to the dashboard and sniffed with mild interest.

"Geothermal springs, that'd be my guess. Planet ain't dead even if most everything on its surface is." She thumped his seat. "Pick up the pace. No time for sightseeing."

Sheni reluctantly pushed the accelerator lever forward, but the rover stayed put. The engine revved, the wheels kicked up a cloud of stones. They went nowhere.

"Curse the gods," Gecki snarled. "What did I *just* say? Watch where you're driving!"

"It's not my fault!" Sheni rammed the lever back and forth. "We must have hit a patch of silt, or something!"

"A patch of...?" Gecki threw back her head and hissed. "Gods, shut the engine off. We're gonna have to dig the rover out ourselves."

"You mean, out there?"

"Yes, out there." Gecki secured her helmet with barely controlled fury. "Unless you want to sit back and wait for a tow-truck to find us."

Sheni only just got his own helmet on before Gecki climbed out the passenger-side door and all the heat got sucked from the cabin. He too dropped from the vehicle, then jumped when he discovered Alan was somehow already outside. Frost speckled his bobble hat.

"Don't wander off," Sheni said, his teeth chattering.

He marched past Alan toward the rear wheels. His claustrophobic helmet made each breath sound flat and horridly close. Gecki stood on the opposite side, inspecting the tyres. Sure enough, they were half-submerged in a small fissure of fine grey dirt. Flecks and pebbles lay scattered across the rover's faint tracks disappearing back into the dark cave.

"Maybe your claws are even stronger than I thought," he shouted to Gecki, "but I don't reckon we can dig those wheels out with our hands alone."

"You're right. Look for some bigger rocks we can jam under the tyres."

"How is piling rocks up like wheel chocks gonna help?"

Gecki rolled her reptilian eyes.

"This is a rover, human. It needs something sturdy to drive over so it can gain traction. A bunch of rocks are hardly going to pose an all-terrain truck much of a problem, are they?"

Sheni turned and searched the cave for rocks he could carry while Gecki stomped off in the opposite direction, muttering to herself. He found a small mound of suitable stones about ten metres away, but the ones that were any use were too big to carry more than two at a time.

He dropped them as the red light bleeding from the rear of the vehicle cut out briefly. It was as if something large had sprinted past the tail lights and blocked their gaze. But apart from the scratching and grunting sounds coming from Gecki's side of the truck, he could have sworn he was alone.

Yeah, screw stretching his legs. He *really* didn't like being outside the rover.

He squeezed the first two rocks behind the tyre on his side of the silt-pit. It was a start, he supposed. Gecki's pile was already bigger, because *of course* it was. He glanced to his right, expecting to still see Alan standing beside the driver's door, wondering if it was worth asking the small guy for help. His blood ran colder than the air turning his breath to steam. The woolly idiot was missing.

Jerking his head to his left, he discovered their small, globular companion standing about twenty-five metres back down the tunnel, staring into the darkness.

"Alan!" he hissed. "What did I just tell you? Stop strolling off where we can't see you!"

Much to Sheni's surprise, Alan immediately turned and sprinted back to the rover, hopping into the cabin and slamming the driver's side door shut behind him.

"How's your pile going?" Gecki asked, making Sheni jump a second time. "Two rocks? Seriously, is that all you've done?"

"What do you think's got Alan so spooked?" he asked, squinting into the darkness.

"I dunno." Gecki shrugged and added another rock to Sheni's pile. "He probably saw a mushroom with the wrong number of spots, or something. Who cares?"

Sheni took a few slow steps backward.

"I think we should..."

Gecki looked at Sheni curiously, then trained her one good eye to peer through the murky shadows. She shook her head in frustration.

"I don't see anything out there."

"Neither do I, but listen..."

They both held their breath, blocking out the gentle trickle from the subterranean waterfall as best they could, concentrating instead on the quiet scraping noise that scratched at the very periphery of hearing, clawing like the desperate rat that still gnawed in Sheni's belly, growing madder and more frenzied the closer it came...

"I think it's time we were leaving," Gecki suddenly rasped, racing Sheni back to the rover.

They clambered inside the cabin, slammed the doors shut, locked them. Gecki screamed at Sheni to hurry up as he fumbled with the straps of his seat. He twisted the ignition key and the engine started. Small miracles, Sheni thought. Alan curled up in the back with his bobble hat pulled down over his bulbous eyes.

"Get us out of here!" Gecki snarled.

Sheni shoved the accelerator lever forward. The tyres spun wildly, kicked up more silt and pebbles. The rover lifted slightly... then sagged back into the narrow pit. Sheni put the rover into reverse, then tried again. It still wouldn't climb out.

"We needed more stones," Gecki rasped irritably.

"Or maybe," Sheni grunted, ramming the lever forward and back, "we shouldn't have piled them up like wheel chocks!"

Something thudded onto the roof of the rover. Sheni and Gecki stopped bickering and looked at one another.

"What was that?" Sheni whispered.

They jumped as another object dropped onto the roof, then a third whacked into the rear of the rover, shaking the sealed doors at the rear of its cargo bed. Alan gurgled out a whimper. Soon the entire vehicle shook from the bombardment, just as it had out in that blasted snowstorm.

Sheni sank into his seat as a set of long, knobbly fingers descended over the top of the windscreen. Something was crawling off the roof. A second hand as emaciated as the first probed the glass. Then came the head.

Grey. Bald. Skin like a plastic bag, so old it's become practically translucent, pulled tight over a basketball. Sunken, eyeless sockets. A round, lipless mouth full of teeth like stalactites, closer in nature to Xotl's beak than anything remotely human.

Another hand curled around the window of the driver-side door, followed by yet another on the windscreen. Nails scratched at the seal between the rear doors. Fists knocked against the undercarriage. The whole rover was crawling with them.

"I thought you said nothing could survive out here," Sheni hissed out the corner of his mouth, his chest hitching with each nervous breath.

Gecki peeled her lips back, bared her sharp, saliva-dripping teeth.

"I guess that depends on your definition of survival..."

Two of the creatures were spread across the windscreen now, and a third had barricaded Sheni's door. At the sound of Gecki's voice, all three of them snapped their sightless heads towards the cabin and screamed. It was a primal scream, a *pained* scream, the high-pitched howl of a predator caught in a trap.

"Drive, Sheni!" Gecki snarled at him.

Sheni rammed the lever forward again, gritted his teeth as the engine revved harder and harder. The rear wheels skidded fruitlessly, and then something caught. He didn't know if it was the rocks they stacked up or if one of the creatures got tangled up in the treads, but the rover shot up from the pit and sped over the cavern floor.

Still the screaming monstrosities clawed at the glass, trying to break through to the fresh meat beneath. The rover's headlights swam across rock pillars and dank cavern walls, each coated with more of the lanky, naked, shrieking fiends.

"I really hope this cave system leads somewhere," Sheni shouted, desperately navigating the charging rover through tunnels, tubes and chambers.

"Don't look at me," Gecki replied. "You're the one who wanted to seek the safety of a godsdamn monster nest!"

The creature hanging onto Sheni's door lost its grip and tumbled into the darkness. A dozen more sprinted after the rover, eager to take its place. They crawled out of every pock and crack in the rock, summoned by the screech of their brethren and the growl of the intruders' engine.

One of them stood upright in the path of the rover. Sheni drove right over it, the wheels barely registering the impact.

"Hey," Gecki rasped. "That look like light to you?"

Half a kilometre ahead was a misshapen oval of perhaps not light, exactly, but at least something less gloomy than the rest of the cave network. It wasn't the warm glow of summer sun, that was for sure. The closer they got to it, the less Sheni needed his headlights.

"Whatever it is, I'm going for it," Sheni said, skidding the rover sideways. "Let's just hope we don't launch ourselves off the side of a mountain, yeah?"

The one remaining ghoul stretched out on the hood of the rover continued to screech and pound at the windshield. To Sheni's horror, its scrabbling fingers found the crack in the glass and tried to pry it open, cutting its flesh and smearing blood as it fought manically to get inside...

Even the meagre light of the cave mouth became blinding as the rover departed the darkness. Sheni squinted, forced himself to keep the accelerator lever pushed as far forward as it would go...

They boosted into the air, weightless for half a second, then landed against the rocks and snow with a clumsy crash. Immediately the winds battered the rover's flanks and tendrils of frost crept across the glass. The creature attacking the rover panicked and writhed from the sudden cold, lost its grip on the jagged glass and was carried off, still lashing out in bloodthirsty distress, into the grey storm.

Sheni and Gecki sat there a moment, their chests rapidly rising and falling, the rover's engine idling, as the chassis lamented the sudden change in exterior pressure. Alan rose to his spindly feet and lifted the woolly hat's trim from his eyes. Behind them, just visible in the side-mirror, the rest of the ghoulish beings paced back and forth along the cavern's threshold.

Deep breath in – hold it – deep breath out. Sheni cracked his knuckles and, under the heat of Gecki's glare, slowly edged the rover forwards again.

"Yes, fine, whatever," he mumbled. "Next time we'll stick to the route."

CHAPTER EIGHT

According to Gecki, the caverns beneath the icy ridge had taken them all the way through the second and third rain (well, snow) band of the Gellar Valley storm, and they were now in the comparatively calmer gulley between the third band and the deadly eyewall.

According to Sheni, however, they were lost. Comparatively calm this section of the Valley might be, but it was still a case of driving blind through either dense blizzards or endless swells of tundra – a choice of white noise, or just plain white.

"Button," was Alan's contribution to their present state of affairs.

Since their ordeal in the caverns, Sheni hadn't deviated from the highlighted NavMap route. Flurries of snow formed grand waves to either side of the rover as it burst through the dunes, but the easier drive wasn't doing much to improve Sheni's mood. His head throbbed from a potent combination of stress and dehydration, and his eyelids grew heavy. He almost didn't register the tattered orange flag billowing from the top of the crooked, rusty antenna jutting out from a rock shaped like a boot. Some old relic, he reckoned, from when outposts like Borel-Six had set up scientific checkpoints to gather data from the storm.

"Another couple of hours and we should reach the spot where the *Lucky Quark* went down," Gecki rasped excitedly.

"Another couple of hours," Sheni grumbled, "and we'll be torn apart by tornadoes and thrown across the valley in a hundred different pieces."

Gecki's grin fell. She looked down her snout at Sheni and snorted.

"What's got *you* so riled up?"

"What's got me riled up?" Sheni stared at her. "I dunno, Gecki! Maybe it's the fact I'm cold, I'm tired, my stomach's rumbling and my throat's parched, I wish I had something strong to drink, my whole body aches, this suit stinks of cabbages and, to be totally frank with you, I need to pee. This whole mission is unbelievably dangerous, and for once it's not me who's put us in this stupid situation but you, the captain who always has a go at me for not thinking things through properly! So yeah, I'm a little on edge, you know? I don't understand what's suddenly come over you, I don't know how we're supposed to survive this freakin' planet, and I just want to go home. And you know what? I don't even know what home *is* anymore! Do I have one? Is it the *Silver Hart*, or Earth, or New Terra? God, I don't know. I give up."

He sagged into his seat and let the rover roll to a stop. Gecki and Alan exchanged a concerned look. Well, one of Alan's eyes met Gecki's. The other was presently scouring the cabin's junction boxes for more wires to unplug.

"If you want to leave the crew, just say it," Gecki rasped impatiently.

"Of course I don't want to leave the crew, you idiot." Sheni ran his hands down his face. Or rather he tried to, realised he still had his helmet on, and grunted in frustration. "I'm just tired of all this, you know? Tired of owing money to awful people, of doing the wrong thing just to get by for a few more rotations, of pretending to myself that one day we're gonna get lucky and everything's gonna change for the better."

Despite clearly wanting to get a move on, Gecki sighed and nodded heavily.

"Yeah, I get that. That's why we've gotta pull off this job. Put all those cruddy decisions behind us." She jabbed a claw at the passenger seat. "Go on, budge. Let me take over for a bit."

"I thought you said you couldn't drive," he mumbled, one eyebrow raised.

"Ah, I've watched you do it. How hard can it be?"

Sheni scoffed, but he undid his straps and climbed out of the driver's seat all the same. Letting Gecki drive the rover for a bit couldn't hurt, could it? She was the one so intent on reaching the damn casino ship, after all. He removed his helmet and bunched his legs up in the seat opposite, trying – and mostly failing – to get comfortable.

"I might just rest my eyes for a bit, actually..."

"Good idea," Gecki said, lurching the rover forwards with clumsy gusto. "A nap's sure to bring out some of that good old Sheni optimism."

He thought he replied with, "Yeah, and we're gonna need it," but the words never left his mouth. Even his head knocking repeatedly against the glass of the passenger-side window wasn't enough to stop him from drifting off.

Soon, that ocean of white outside the rover faded to black.

SHADOWS IN THE SNOW

He woke to the sound of thick snow crunching under big tyres.

"How long was I out?" he asked, rubbing a knuckle into his eye.

"Couple of hours," Gecki replied, not glancing over from the driver's seat. "Gonna be coming up on the hurricane's eyewall any time now."

"Oh, great," he groaned. "Glad I haven't missed the best part."

A ragged streak of flapping orange fabric to the left of the rover caught his attention.

"Erm, Gecki? You saw that, right?"

"What, the flags? Yeah. Each time I pass one, the NavMap tells me to hang a right. Reckon they're pointing the way."

Sheni closed his eyes, set his jaw, and exhaled slowly.

"And are they *all* set in rocks shaped like a big shoe?"

"Can't say I've paid that much attention," she replied, squinting through the snowstorm.

Sheni reached over to the NavMap's touchscreen and pinched his fingers together to zoom out.

"For crying out loud, you stupid lizard – you've been driving in a massive circle for two hours!"

"What? No." Gecki glanced down at the screen, then threw back her head in frustration. "Well, how in the stars was I supposed to know? I'm just going where the NavMap tells me!"

"You didn't ever think to stop and check the route?"

"The passenger is the navigator, you know that. And *someone* decided to have themselves a little sleep, didn't they?"

Gecki slowed the rover to a halt, then left her seat and inspected one of the junction boxes in the ceiling of the cabin. A charred rectangular box clattered to the floor when she opened the panel.

"Navigation unit's busted," she growled.

Sheni turned to Alan, who stood in the corner with his arms sticking out from his coat's rigid sleeves like uncooked spaghetti.

"Did you do this?"

Alan gurgled innocently.

"Nah, it's not his fault." Gecki tossed the navigation unit in her hand. "It almost certainly blew when the storm rolled us over. Or those freaks in the caverns did it. The outside of the rover's probably ripped to pieces."

"How do we fix it?"

"We don't." Gecki dropped the unit back onto the floor with a *clang* and returned to the driver's seat. "Rover needs a new one. Doesn't matter. We'll just have to drive blind."

"Blinder than we already are?" Sheni yelled, gesturing to the blizzard outside the windows.

"We still have access to the map," she said, jabbing at the screen with a claw, "just not the route. We'll just head" – she swung her claw from the screen to the snowstorm outside – "that way."

"But without the navigation unit," Sheni screamed in mounting disbelief, "how do you know if that way *is* that way?"

"I don't, all right?" she snarled, ramming the accelerator lever forward. "But we're not getting any closer to the casino by letting the rover get swallowed in snow!"

"Come on Xotl, pick up." Sheni tried calling the *Silver Hart* again, but the comm unit wouldn't connect. "Stars above. Signal's even worse than before. Without that navigation unit, there's no chance we'll find our way back to Borel-Six, either. Though I suppose you *could* be driving west right now, for all *you* know."

"Oh, the human thinks he can do better, does he?"

"Yes, honestly! Which one of us has proven they can drive in a straight line, and which—"

"Shut up, Sheni. Don't you see that?"

For a second or two, no, he didn't. Then he caught a short glimpse as the snowfall subsided for a moment – a soft, phosphorescent glow about a mile or so away. A yellow-orange colour, it came and went, on and off, like a cigarette lighter being repeatedly sparked.

"Are you sure it's not just the same flag again?" Sheni grunted through gritted teeth.

"Stop being stupid. It's a light, and you know it. Just like the one outside the airlock hatch for Borel-Six."

"There aren't any outposts in the Gellar Valley," Sheni reminded her. "Even that research checkpoint we passed probably doesn't work anymore. Nobody comes out this way, right?"

"Well something did, coz that ain't natural."

The blinking light bled brighter across the falling flurry as the rover punched through the settled snow. He remembered what he first thought about the similar bulb outside the outpost, that it was like the beacon of a lighthouse back on Earth. Those beacons hadn't been designed to attract ships but to keep them from crashing onto the rocks.

"Yeah, it ain't natural," Sheni repeated cautiously. "So is the smart move to drive toward it, or away?"

CHAPTER NINE

Gecki crawled the rover toward the flashing light. It belonged to the top of a pole that had been thrust deep into the snow like a javelin. The cold, snow-swallowed metal hull of a crashed ship glowed a hot orange under its blinking gaze. Definitely not the *Lucky Quark*. It was smaller than the *Silver Hart*, even, but slightly larger than a drop ship. A cargo shuttle, perhaps. Its nose was crumpled against the rocks and its charred thrusters had suffered damage to their heat sinks.

"Careful," Sheni said, his hand shooting across the cabin to grab Gecki's arm. "There's someone out there."

A dark figure in thick winter clothes had emerged from a crevice in the ship's flank and was waving their arms from side to side above their head. Sheni guessed they could see into the rover's cabin. Confident that Gecki and Sheni had seen them, too, the figure beckoned for them to enter the ship.

"Looks like they're inviting us in," Gecki rasped. "I'll back us up."

"I thought we were in a hurry to get to the *Quark* before

the Kilonova Corporation," Sheni said through gritted teeth.

"Like you said, we've got no idea which direction we're going without a navigation unit," she replied. "And who knows? Maybe this person can point us the right way."

"Oh, yes. Because clearly somebody stranded in the middle of the worst storm in a hundred star systems is an expert on giving directions."

Gecki reversed the rover until it was almost touching the crack in the ship's half-buried hull, then killed the engine. Together with the surrounding rocks, the ship had created a sort of wind breaker, shielding them from the worst of the blizzard. Still, Sheni re-attached his helmet to his suit. The cabin had cultivated quite a toasty temperature since they left the caverns, which would be lost the second they unlocked its rear doors.

Sheni snatched the key from the ignition and pocketed it while Gecki wasn't looking. After this little pit stop, it would probably be best if he took the wheel again.

"Ready?" Gecki asked Sheni and Alan, her hand on the bolts keeping the doors shut.

"Not at all," Sheni replied. "We're heading inside a derelict ship to meet a complete stranger, and we have nothing to defend ourselves with. I don't think this is a smart idea, you know?"

"They might have a toilet."

"A good point, well made. Hold my hand, Alan. It's only a couple of metres from here to the ship, but we don't want you blowing away."

Gecki swung the rear doors open. Snowflakes immediately fluttered inside. Sheni hopped down to the ground first and helped Alan disembark. Gecki slammed the doors shut behind them and then together they squeezed through the crevice in single file.

The ship was just as orange and red on the inside as it was out, but none of the ship's lights were on. A fire burned in the centre of the cargo hold's floor. The wind wailed outside, but in here the air was smoky and still. The ship itself leaned on a slight downward gradient, but its occupant had piled the fire's cinders and old rags higher on one side to keep it upright.

The occupant in question stood half a dozen metres away from the crevice, nervously flexing the fingers of their thick leather gloves. Not an inch of their body wasn't covered by their dense, fleecy overcoat, their wind-bleached thermal trousers and their tight black snood. They were about five foot six and vaguely humanoid in shape, in that they stood upright and had what Sheni considered a regular amount of limbs.

They tried to speak but their voice came out muffled. They flung back their hood and pulled off their goggles. Underneath was a petite face covered in shimmering turquoise scales, a pair of big, black eyes, and slitted nostrils that flared in rhythm with their words.

"Gods, it's been so long since I've seen anyone," she said, stumbling over her words. "You are real, aren't you? Do you need to get warm? Please, sit down. I'm Fin, by the way. Fin Sheylus."

Gecki removed her helmet, sniffed the air cautiously, and then cast a curious yellow eye over their host.

"Nice to meet you," she rasped slowly. "I'm Gecki, this is Sheni, and that little guy staring straight into the flames is Alan."

Gecki joined Alan by the fire, pulled him another foot away to be safe. Sheni lingered by the crevice a moment longer, shifting his weight from one snowy boot to another.

"Sorry if this seems like a weird question," he asked, "but, erm, where around here do you go to the bathroom?"

"Oh, yeah." Fin's face brightened. "It's just through that door and on your right. Water recycler's on a closed loop, so... you know. It'll flush. Just give it a couple whacks if it starts to freeze."

The rest of the ship was lit only by neon sticks Fin had snapped in half and scattered along the floor. The primary power systems were offline. Only a few emergency subroutines remained operational. Finding the bathroom was a lot easier than removing the relevant components of his suit so he could actually use it. By the time he returned to the ship's cargo hold, Gecki and Fin were already deep in conversation.

"What happened to your ship?" Gecki asked, as Sheni squatted down and warmed his face by the fire.

"It, erm... well, it crashed," Fin replied, giving them a pained smile. "We were on our way to Borel-Three. Scheduled supply run, happens once a quarter. Aeril took us too low, I guess. We lost control as we hit the storm, and, well" – she gestured to the wreckage – "here I am."

"What happened to Aeril?" Sheni asked.

Fin simply shook her head.

"She said the storm wouldn't be too bad," Fin continued. "That it was coming up to a quote-unquote 'tranquil' period. I'm guessing she forgot to take relativity into account, though. She never did wrap her head around gravitational time dilation, what with coming from such a dense planet and all."

Sheni raised an eyebrow in Gecki's direction as if to say, *Maybe you calculated wrong, too*, but the lizard ignored him.

"How long have you been out here alone?" she asked Fin.

"Coming up to a month, I think. Good thing we were carrying so much food, right?" Fin nodded to the crates stacked up on the other side of the cargo hold. "I would have starved to death otherwise. Oh! Where are my manners? Can I get you anything to eat?"

"We're fine, thanks," Gecki said, tilting her head.

"Don't be silly, I've got loads to spare." Fin hurried over to the crate closest to the cockpit and frantically rummaged around inside. She glanced over her shoulder, then returned with a bundle of protein paste-packets and tin water bottles.

"Have a drink, at least," she said, handing them out enthusiastically. "You must be shattered after such a long drive. Nice rover you've got out there. Did you come all the way from Six?"

"Six?" The cork of Sheni's water slipped out without friction. "Oh, *Borel*-Six. Yeah. How'd you guess?"

"Closest outpost." Fin shrugged and flashed an awkward smile. "What are you guys even doing, driving all the way out here? Not that I'm complaining, mind you. I thought I was dead for sure."

Gecki shared a glance with Sheni, who was glugging down water like an unplugged bathtub, before she answered.

"Admit it. You and your friend thought you'd try your luck at breaking into the *Lucky Quark*, didn't you?"

Fin looked at all three of them sheepishly. Alan was already three protein bars deep. She shrugged, embarrassed.

"Well, Aeril said it was worth a try. It was all her idea, really – I'd never even heard of that place before she brought it up. But we were scheduled to come this way anyway, so I reckoned, why not? Anything to quit the shuttle business for good."

Fin's black eyes grew to engulf half her head. Her mouth, like that of a guppy's, formed a perfect circle of surprise.

"Wait, if you're here, then... then was Aeril right about the Gellar Valley storm dying down for a bit? Enough to drive a rover through, at least?" Fin rubbed a gloved hand down her scaly face. "Gods. You've got to take me to Six so I can ping the company for rescue!"

"Not so fast," Gecki snarled, taking a swig of her own drink. "Your friend might have got her numbers wrong, but the *Lucky Quark* is still out there. We ain't heading back till we've got our hands on what she's holding."

"Please," Fin pleaded. "We have to leave before we're stuck in this valley for good!"

"You're welcome to ride with us," Sheni said, having to actively stretch his face to keep from nodding off. It had to be the long drive coupled with the crackling warmth of the fire. "We can take you back to Borel-Six when we return the rover. Or you can stay here and wait for the next truck to come this way."

"You three are crazy." Fin sighed. "But I guess I'll have to take you up on that offer. I don't see me receiving any better ones, not before the storm picks back up again. And these supplies won't last another three months, let alone fifteen years."

"Good choice." Sheni reclined next to Alan, who was snoring through the fluffy collar of his coat. "We can decide which direction we're going later. For now, Alan and I are going to take a little nap."

Gecki growled at them impatiently. "I take it you haven't

seen anyone from Kilonova pass through here?" she asked Fin.

"No. Like I said, you're the first people I've seen since my ship went down. Haven't heard from anyone either since none of my transmissions are going through."

"Then we're still ahead of the strike force for now." Gecki rose to her feet in a huff. "One hour, Sheni, and then we're heading to the *Quark*. If you're coming with us, Fin, then you do exactly as I say, got it?"

Fin nodded enthusiastically.

"Right." Gecki sniffed the air again. "I'm off to take a leak."

"First door on the right," Sheni mumbled, waving his hand.

Fin's gloves were scrambling over Sheni's enviro-suit the second Gecki entered the bathroom. Sheni lifted his head, groggy and confused.

"I'm sorry," the turquoise alien said, "but I'm not going any deeper into this storm. You guys are as stupid as Aeril. So hungry for credits, you'll die getting them. Well, you won't take me with you."

Sheni rolled his head to the right. Between him and Alan were two near-empty bottles of water, plus the squeezed wrappers of all the protein pastes Alan had scoffed down. The drinks. He remembered how easily the corks had come out. Like the seal was already broken. She must have put some kind of sleep aid in them.

Fin found the ignition key in the front compartment of his chest plate. She inspected it in the light cast by the fire, then clasped it tightly and stood up so she loomed over Sheni's inert body.

She jumped at a sharp *clang*, followed by a sustained metallic groan. The rest of the ship was empty. Just the hull flexing from the difference between internal and external temperatures.

"Your friend has probably passed out in the bathroom," she said, backing away towards the crevice. "Don't worry, the sedative'll wear off in an hour or two. The settlers use it to treat insomnia, apparently. I promise to let the people at Six know you're out here. Maybe they'll send a rescue team. I really hope they do, honest."

A sudden squelching sound interrupted the fire's steady crackle. Fin arched her back and gawped wordlessly. The ignition key fell from her rigid, outstretched hand.

"Stupid, are we?" Gecki rasped wickedly, her camouflage gradually vanishing from head to toe as her bare scales returned to their natural mint-green colour. "Not as stupid as thinking chloral hydrate works on reptilians."

She let Fin's body drop heavily to the metal floor, then flicked her wrist to get the blue-green blood off her claws.

"What did you do that for?" Sheni groaned, the words feeling like mashed potato in his mouth.

"Fin was stealing our rover, you idiot. I'm guessing that was her plan from the moment she saw us drive up through the snow. She dosed those drinks long before we mentioned going to the *Lucky Quark*, that's for sure."

"But you didn't need to *kill* her, you horrid lizard."

"Oh, shut up. You're so freaking soft these days. What do you think would have happened if she'd gotten away with our wheels? Yeah, that's right. All three of us would be dead. Better one than three, whichever way you look at it."

She shivered. Her hot breath created a chimney of steam.

"Gods, it's cold. Gotta get back in that suit, pronto."

Sheni must have fallen asleep, because the next thing he

knew a reinforced boot was being kicked into his ribs. Gecki was dressed again and holding a large grey box.

"Get up. You can be drugged and delirious in the rover."

"What's that under your arm?"

"The navigation unit from Fin's ship. She won't be needing it anymore."

"Stars above." He propped himself up on his elbows despite the agony of a dozen knitting needles being stabbed through his parietal lobe. "Did you always plan to kill her and steal her equipment?"

"No, I *planned* to ask her for this nicely in exchange for saving her life. Would have been a pretty good deal for her, seeing as her ship was already totalled. Her choice. Now, get in the freakin' rover."

Sheni stumbled upright and fought not to vomit. God knows how long he stood there, hunched over with his hands on his thighs. When he eventually summoned the courage to open his eyes again, praying the ship had taken a break from spinning, Alan was also on his spindly feet beside him, his bobble hat on straight, his eyes wide and wonky, and only looking as green as he normally did.

"Rover," Gecki snarled from the crevice. "Now!"

Sheni's stuffy helmet made his stomach turn. He desperately wished he could rub his face in the snow, but he didn't fancy losing his nose to frostbite. The second he and Alan were safely back inside the rover, he removed his helmet once again and resumed a horizontal position on the extremely uncomfortable floor.

Gecki slammed the navigation unit down beside him.

"Alan," she rasped. "I don't care how you do it, but get this thing wired up, will you?"

Sheni barely registered the subsequent clanging, sizzling and occasional giggle as Alan gleefully got to work.

This unit was easily ten times the size of the rover's original model. No way would it fit back in the junction box. The next time he opened his eyes, the navigation unit was dangling from the ceiling by a pair of fraying wires, swinging unsteadily beside his head like a medieval battering ram suspended on chains.

"Nice work, Alan," Sheni vaguely remembered mumbling, shooting his diminutive crew mate a thumbs-up before fading back into unconsciousness.

CHAPTER TEN

Sheni woke up when the dangling navigation unit swung into the side of his head. He groaned and pushed it away like it was the snooze button on an alarm clock. It responded by knocking into his head again, harder this time.

He pushed through his paralysing hangover and propped himself up on his elbows. His forehead felt heavy and unyielding, as if someone had coated it with lead. The rover was bleating out the same shrill complaint over and over again. Warning signs had popped up across its dashboard like warts on a plague victim.

"Oh, God," he said, rubbing his temples. "What the hell is happening?"

Alan's head popped up from the passenger seat in front of him.

"High-celerity dismantlement," he gurgled.

"Maybe it's easier to understand Alan when my brain has been scrambled like eggs," Sheni moaned, blowing out his cheeks to keep from emptying his stomach, "but that doesn't sound good."

"But it's not *bad*," Gecki rasped stubbornly, jerking the rover's directional lever to the right. "Not yet."

Sheni pointed a wavering finger at a dashboard lit up like a Christmas tree.

"What about those warning signs, then?"

"That's all warning signs are, though, right? Warnings. Nothing's actually gone wrong yet, not *really*. They're just there to let us know something *could*."

"Yeah, course." He smiled with diminishing delirium. "More like advice, you know?"

"Exactly. There's that unique brand of Sheni optimism I remember!"

Sheni removed Alan from the passenger seat and strapped himself in. The tiny mechanic went back to inspecting and rewiring all of the cabin's remaining junction boxes.

"How long until we reach the eyewall?"

"Oh, yeah, about that." Gecki turned her head. She had a mad look in her cold, milky eye. "We're already in it. I'd say we're maybe, erm, halfway through."

The rover lurched to the left, and for a second Sheni was sure its metal tyres weren't churning through anything at all. It bounded forward, bumped clumsily off a jagged shard of ice, and then drifted in a counter-clockwise semi-circle. Gecki was hardly driving it anymore, just micro-adjusting the direction of its skids as the storm dragged it one way or the other.

A yellow-white lightning bolt pierced through the thick shroud of hail and struck a gnarly rock formation only a couple of dozen metres to their right.

"Turn back, Gecki," Sheni yelled, suddenly feeling remarkably sober. He could still see the bolt tattooed on his retinas. "Fin was right about one thing, you know. You're gonna get all of us killed."

"There's no point in turning back now," Gecki replied, baring her teeth. "We're halfway. It's just as quick to push all the way to the other side!"

"No, it's not, you maniac! We'll still have to drive back through it afterwards!"

"Sunk cost fallacy," Alan said, giggling like they were riding a carousel.

He flipped open a panel and pulled out a wire. All of the rover's alarms shut up.

"Thank you, Alan," Sheni and Gecki shouted together, both louder than they intended to be.

More lightning flashed in the distance, each time providing a brief snapshot of the maelstrom's innards. This was far worse than the hurricane's earlier snow band. For the first time since setting off, Sheni was glad the steering levers weren't in his hands. It wasn't just the chunks of ice hurtling through the air that worried him, or the risk of being fried by lightning, or even the not altogether ridiculous idea that the wind might pluck their rover off the ground and lob it across the mountains. The terrain itself was lethal enough, moulded into ugly, treacherous shapes by relentless natural forces no species had yet the audacity to harness.

One such chunk of ice crashed into the windscreen. The existing crack in the glass grew wider, longer, threatened to splinter out like a spider's web and shatter completely. Another collided with the right-hand flank of the rover. Sheni gulped and tugged on his straps. The resulting dent in the external paneling was deep enough to be seen from inside. Hell, the ice lodged in their vehicle's flank was mere millimetres away from poking through and dripping on the cabin's floor.

"Not far now," Gecki snarled defiantly, tapping the NavMap screen with a claw. The geometric map spun and flipped, the green arrows resetting every few seconds. The storm was messing with the planet's electromagnetic signals, Sheni reckoned. The guidance system hadn't a clue which way was north or south. They'd been no worse off driving without a navigation unit at all.

"Oh, good." Sheni sank further into his seat. "Here come the tornadoes."

Out of the swirling greyness they howled, black winds full of hungry smoke. Each time the world froze in an electrostatic snapshot, Sheni counted another one born from the void. Three. No, four – no, *five*. Each one forming a twisting pillar bridging the dark heavens and snow-swallowed earth. Each one carving trenches through an already ravaged wasteland.

"Is this rover built to handle one of those?" he yelled at Gecki, as the hull continued to groan.

"I mean, I assume it would rather we kept our distance," she replied, doing her best to direct the rover away from the path of the closest tornado.

Sheni watched the twister in question tear a chunk of rock free from the hard earth and hurl it as casually as one might throw a baseball.

"We need to find a way to ground ourselves," he shouted. "You know, make the rover heavier!"

"What do you expect me to do, throw down a freakin' anchor? We're getting to that casino ship, Sheni. One way or the other, we're going through."

The flying chunk of rock finally shattered into pebbles against the side of a craggy tor.

"I'd just prefer it if we could get through on the ground," Sheni hissed through gritted teeth, "rather than through the air."

Something exploded inside one of the tornadoes. A spark from a lightning strike; the fuel tank of a downed ship igniting. Sheni didn't know how it happened, only that he was now looking at a towering inferno, a writhing spire of fire and fury.

Alan slowly came into view between the two seats, staring up at the bright flames with his big, bulging eyes and cooing with awe and admiration.

"Wonderful. Brilliant." Sheni laughed in dry and defeated disbelief. "So we'll be incinerated before we get tossed into the side of a mountain. I suppose we should be grateful we won't feel the crash."

"Burning alive is definitely worse than a sudden, traumatic impact," Gecki replied distractedly, wrenching the levers to the right as the rover skidded through another snow dune. "This is not an improvement."

"Thanks, Gecki." He ducked as a block of ice flew over the roof of the rover, then hastily reattached his helmet. "Just concentrate on not getting us killed, will ya?"

The wheels found rock and dirt, and the renewed traction allowed Gecki to just about thread the rover between the first and second cyclones. The vehicle skidded towards the left, then back towards the right, as each tornado clasped them in its grip. For a moment precisely halfway between the two, the backside of the rover lifted into the air, its rear tyres spinning helplessly as its front pair coasted along without power, before it crashed back down to the ground with a driveshaft-breaking crunch.

What should have been a moment of triumph only

terrified Sheni more. He couldn't see an end to the storm. No eye of serenity. No exit. Just more vortex, more tornadoes, more lightning bolts blasting black craters in the snow.

A shuddering groan from the dented panel behind him made Sheni twist around in his seat. It was beginning to peel free.

He undid his straps and staggered into the rear of the cabin. He checked the gloves of his enviro-suit. They looked thick enough to protect his fingers from sharp metal. Hopefully. He grabbed the dented panel and pulled hard, fighting against the wrestling winds outside.

Gurgles to his right. Sheni squinted through the strain. Alan was standing beside him, tugging on the panel with his weedy spaghetti arms, producing about as much force as an air freshener hanging from a rear-view mirror.

"The rover's gonna be torn apart if we stay here much longer," he screamed, struggling to be heard above the rising whistle of air blasting through the growing gap.

"I'm pushing it as fast as it'll go," Gecki snarled back. "It's not like I want to be in this hellscape any longer than you do!"

A blast from the rapidly spinning pillar of fire engulfed the left flank of the rover and cast the interior of the vehicle in angry red light. The heat was immense. Sweat dripped from Sheni's forehead and splattered against his visor. Gecki banked the rover to the right, and the dented panel almost swung off completely. Sheni quickly yanked it back into position before he or Alan could be sucked out.

"We've got to be close, right? How far are we from the *Quark's* last known coordinates?"

"Close."

"Close like we're just around the corner," he asked, the panel shaking in his hands like the handlebar of a particularly wobbly shopping cart, "or close like the eye of the storm's another ten kilometres away?"

"I don't know, Sheni, all right? But I'm pretty close to putting a claw through your eye socket if you don't quit asking me questions!"

The hot path of the flaming twister had melted the snow to slush, and the sub-zero temperature rushing back in its wake had then frozen the water rock solid. The rover's tyres lost all grip. They skidded down the icy river, spinning slowly, the view outside the window growing even more nauseating than before.

Then the rover hit snow again, almost rolled onto its side with Sheni dangling from the cabin's wall like it were the ceiling, and suddenly they were careening forward again, through the increasingly disparate herd of tornadoes...

"Erm, Gecki?" Sheni leaned backward from the shaking panel. "Those rocks... do they look like an edge to you?"

A wall of grey-blue rock lay directly ahead of them, its jagged lip curving upwards into a misshapen ramp. He couldn't see what awaited them on the other side. His gut told him the answer was a big fat nothing.

"Gecki?"

"Quit your cry-babying," she snarled. "You wanted out of this storm, didn't you?"

"Stars above... Alan, hold on tight!"

Alan let go of the quaking panel and instead clutched his loose button close to his chest.

"That's not what I meant, you—!"

The rover clattered into the rocks and took off. Sheni slammed into the wall of the cabin and let go of the panel, which was immediately snatched away by the storm. He became weightless as the vehicle twisted through the air. Alan tumbled through the hole shortly after, despite Sheni's desperate attempt to grab his flying crew mate, and then the hood of the rover bulldozed into the frozen dirt.

CHAPTER ELEVEN

The world was white.

Is this the afterlife? Sheni wondered. He felt numb, like he was just an essence, a construct with no body. There was nobody to talk to and nothing to do. If this was heaven, or some other extraterrestrial alternative, he was already bored of it.

Then he heard the muffled crumpling of snow under heavy boots and realised he was just lying face down on the floor. *Now* his body decided to ache from the crash. Parts of him certainly wished he was dead.

He lifted his right arm and sluggishly wiped the clumps of snow from his visor. His helmet wasn't cracked, thank the stars. He was damn cold, though. Cold enough to not feel his extremities anymore. He figured some of the life support systems in his suit had taken a nasty hit.

Gecki squatted down on her haunches beside him and prodded his arm with a gloved claw.

"Still got all your limbs?" she asked.

"Where's Alan?" he replied, remembering a green blur

flying out of the hole where the hull should have been. "Is he all right?"

"Alan? Yeah, he's fine. Lost his button when he fell out the rover, but then he found it again, so all's right with the world."

"I think Alan is a grape." Sheni let his head fall back onto the snow. "You can drop them from really high, and they just bounce. Small things lack kinetic energy, or whatever."

"Is that so?" Gecki rasped impatiently. "Come on, get up. We've got work to do."

"Work to do?" Sheni snorted as he climbed to his feet. "What's the point? The rover's busted, you maniac. We're gonna die out here..."

His words trailed off as he spotted the colossal vessel embedded in the snowy earth in front of him. It was almost too large to notice, the way it blocked his entire view of the horizon, and at first he dismissed it as a huge monument of jagged obsidian. But it was a ship, all right, from the protruding, half-shattered bridge right down to the stadium-sized ion thruster pointing diagonally up at the dark, turbulent sky.

The storm had stripped the *Quark* of a great deal of its external heat shields, and an entire upper deck looked to have snapped off at some point during the crash, but otherwise the ship was mostly intact. Alan stood facing it about a dozen metres ahead of them, his arms outstretched as if measuring it, or trying to give the broken giant a hug.

"Stars above," Sheni muttered as he broke into a toothy grin. "We found it. We actually *found* it!"

"First people to set eyes on the *Lucky Quark* since she crashed," Gecki rasped with a proud flourish. "First people to make it through the Gellar Valley storm alive in more than fifteen years, too."

"Yeah, well, we still need to make that trip a second time, remember? And that rover definitely ain't our ticket out of here."

"That's a problem for later. Right now, we've got a casino to loot."

Sheni clapped and rubbed his hands together. This whole heist was a damn disaster, but they weren't down and out quite yet. They'd figure out an escape plan. They always did, right? He just had to stay positive. That and not run headfirst into trouble without thinking, you know, like he used to do.

"We might be stuck in the eye of a deadly storm with no means of escape," he said brightly, "but at least we'll die the richest people for a dozen systems. After you, Captain."

"Richest people for a dozen systems," Gecki repeated. Sheni watched her lick her teeth behind her visor. "Yeah, I sure like the sound of that."

They trudged through the snow – thick swathes of white powder that rose to their knees in places. The air in the eye was unnervingly still, as if not only had the world frozen, but time along with it. Sheni grabbed Alan's outstretched hand as they passed and dragged him along like a kid pulling a sled uphill.

"Man, I bet this ship was impressive in its time."

"Wait until you see the inside," Gecki replied. "Even without the vault, I bet there's enough valuables on board to leave us set for life."

Sheni's stomach fell.

"How many people were on board when the *Quark* crashed?"

Gecki's pace slowed slightly. He guessed she hadn't given that aspect of the heist much thought until now, either.

"Must have been a few thousand, minimum," she answered. "Ship this size needs a big crew, even with so many of its systems automated. It was a pretty popular casino, too. Not the fanciest, not by a long shot, but it followed a popular route. It was reported as a major tragedy on the extranet, so yeah, quite a few casualties."

"Which means a lot of dead bodies."

Sheni slowed almost to a stop. Gecki turned to face him. Alan bumped into the back of his leg.

"You've seen corpses before, Sheni," she rasped. "It'll be grim, yeah. But we didn't cause this crash. We're not even stealing from them, probably, just the company. Turning back now won't honour the dead, and the last thing those bodies care about is somebody letting themselves into that vault."

"Yeah, I know. I just... I'd just been thinking of this as an empty ship, you know? Not a grave site."

"You and me both. But the Kilonova Corporation is on its way. They'll take care of the bodies, give closure to the families and all that. All we need to think about is the credits."

"Just promise me we won't disturb them. That we won't go rummaging around in any corpses' pockets just so we don't leave empty handed."

Gecki nodded slowly.

"Deal. We only take what's in the vault, or at least what's not pinned down elsewhere in the ship. Now, keep moving. If we're not gone before Kilonova arrives, there'll be three more bodies for their strike team to report."

Sheni spotted the name of the ship bolted across its hull in enormous alien runes. For some reason he'd thought it would be written in English. Old habits. His translator chip did a half-decent job at deciphering written language as well as spoken, but he had to concentrate and it tended to give humans a headache. Before the crash, those runes would have been lit up in glorious neon, its light beckoning gamblers from all across the cosmos. Now they were as dull and dead as everything else in the valley.

"How do we even get inside something like this?" Sheni asked. "It's not like crashed ships have front doors."

"That is a good question," Gecki replied. They were walking beside the ship now, and she rapped her knuckles against the cold steel. "Most of the hull will be too thick to cut through. I'm sure some parts of it tore open in the impact."

"But that's not what you're looking for," Sheni guessed.

"Nah. Easy to get lost that way, end up in a dead-end room with no other way out. Last resort."

"And the *first* resort?"

"Airlock," she said, shrugging simply. "Failing that, a service hangar. I had a peek at the ship's schematics on the way to Gressil Prime. What little was freely available on the net, at any rate. The simplest entrance points are usually the best."

"How are we supposed to get an airlock door open when the ship has no power? Even the emergency override switch on the outside won't work."

Gecki pulled a small, handheld plasma torch from the suit compartment on her hip and triggered its blue flame in two short bursts.

"We make our own emergency override," she snarled, clearly pleased with herself.

They stopped walking approximately halfway down the length of the ship and looked up. Yep, that was an airlock, all right – about thirty metres above their heads. A small square of red metal and a thin strip of reinforced glass in a sheer wall of dull, tarnished grey.

A series of rusty, icy rungs formed a ladder scaling the side of the *Quark*. It carried on past the door towards the upper decks. What remained of them, anyway.

"Well, the airlock wasn't gonna be on the underside of the ship, was it?" Gecki rasped, knocking the snow off one of the lowest rungs.

"What if we fall?" Sheni asked. "We don't all bounce like Alan."

"Then the snow will cushion your landing," Gecki replied, already climbing. Her implication that Sheni would be the one doing the falling wasn't lost on him.

"Hop up, Alan," he said, crouching so Alan could ride piggyback.

Just don't look down, he told himself. *Think of all the credits waiting for you inside.*

Thank the stars for his gloves, because the ice would have ripped the skin from his fingers if he'd gripped those rungs with his bare hands. He took his time climbing up after Gecki, who scaled the ladder with relative ease. There was no rush, not for him. He'd only be left dangling from the rungs while Gecki cut through the airlock anyway.

His boot slipped as the rung didn't quite slot into the groove between its heel and toes. He fell slightly, bashed his knee against the hull, and almost lost his grip on the rungs above. Alan's arms tightened around his neck like a noose.

"You okay down there?" Gecki rasped, peering down at them over her shoulder.

"Peachy," Sheni shouted back up while kicking out his feet to find purchase. "Freakin' peachy."

Gecki drew level with the airlock and once more

retrieved the plasma torch from her suit. It hissed like an angry serpent. Golden sparks rained past Sheni as she slowly cut a circle into the airlock door. By the time she was done, Sheni was only a couple of rungs below her, his arms looped around the ladder for good measure.

She returned the torch to her suit, reached across to her smouldering handiwork, and yanked at the handle in its centre. The round panel scraped loose with a shrill shriek that made Sheni wish he could cover his ears. Gecki let it drop to the snowy rocks below.

"In we go," she said excitedly.

She slithered through the opening, remained there while first Alan and then Sheni climbed across. Once safely inside, he leaned against the wall and caught his breath, grateful to be on solid ground again, even if it was listing to one side. Being an airlock, the interior door still blocked their path, but Gecki made even shorter work of that than its exterior counterpart. Once more the red-hot metal fell away from its frame and clanged heavily against the dark and dusty floor beyond. They waited a moment, then quietly crawled through.

"Flashlights on," Gecki whispered. "I doubt there'll be many working generators on board. And I don't want anyone falling down any holes. I don't have enough arms to carry you *and* all the credits."

"Oh, don't worry. I'm fully aware of which you'd leave behind."

Sheni handed his spare flashlight to Alan, despite the oddball's tendency to shine the beam up at his own face as if he were telling campfire ghost stories rather than use it to navigate his surroundings. When he activated his own, the sudden burst of light revealed a plain, unexciting room with a row of storage closets with plastic doors on the left and a security desk complete with computer terminal on the right. Electronic posters were installed on the walls, but without power they were blank. There wasn't a single golden Buddha statue or one-armed bandit in sight.

"Not as glamorous as I expected," Sheni mumbled.

"This isn't the casino, you idiot. As decks go, this one's still fairly low down. This is maintenance, most likely. Some kind of staff level, for sure. The guests and gamblers would have received a much flashier welcome."

The hull clunked and groaned. Sheni cast the beam of his flashlight in the direction of the noise, then jumped as it washed over a humanoid skeleton slumped behind the desk. A security guard, by the look of their uniform. Their bones had been picked relatively clean.

At least the ship's rat population had survived, if nobody else.

Either that or something had gotten in.

"Yeah, well, the casino's where all the credits got spent, isn't it?" He suppressed a shudder. "So how about we make our way upstairs, yeah? This place is giving me the creeps."

"Sheni, you read my mind."

They left the room, passing through security checkpoints that no longer scanned, under electronic signposts that no longer gave directions, down corridors as lifeless and barebones as the unlucky guard by the airlock. Gecki was right – they'd definitely entered the ship on a staff-only level. Computer labs, security offices, one of the ship's numerous generator rooms. Everything was covered in a layer of dust that mimicked the deep snow outside. Neglected pipes dripped and rubbery tubing squeaked. They didn't stumble across any more bodies, but that didn't mean the dead weren't piled up just out of sight. It wasn't as if Sheni dared shine his flashlight through the window of each locked door for very long.

The beam of his flashlight trembled. If those ghoulish freaks had managed to survive in the caverns, who was to say they hadn't somehow found their way out here?

Gecki stomped ahead, not nearly as trepidatious around corpses and derelict spaceships as Sheni, searching for the stairwell that would lead them to the casino floor. She wasn't exactly sure where the management kept the vault, or even if the digital currency was logged and banked in the same place as the physical credit reserves, but the section of the ship where all the money came and went seemed a good place to start.

They found the stairwell – a clunky iron number with numerous steps that had warped in the crash – but Gecki suddenly pulled Sheni into the open doorway of a private workstation instead. Alan continued to waddle down the corridor, swinging his flashlight like an orchestra conductor's baton, until Sheni grabbed him by the hand and yanked him into cover too, just in case.

"Someone's coming," Gecki whispered, furious. "Gods, we're too late..."

A female humanoid – Kerulian most likely, but it was hard to tell given the thick, hooded parka-style jacket she wore – descended from the floor above. She wielded a bulky flashlight of her own. Each footstep rang out like a hammer on an anvil, no matter how cautiously she stepped. She paused on the short landing, squatting and inspecting the deserted corridor with her torch, before creeping down the rest of the stairs. In her other hand she held a data pad like a walkie-talkie.

"I'm telling you, I heard something down here," she whispered.

"It's just gonna be vermin, Lerrin," replied the voice on the other end of the comms.

"Yeah, maybe. I'm still going to check it out."

Gecki raised a claw as level with her mouth as her helmet allowed. *Quiet.* They waited a few seconds for the tapping of nervous footsteps to grow closer. Then Gecki leapt out from the doorway and pinned the woman against the wall directly opposite. She screamed. Her flashlight and data pad clattered to the floor.

Gecki raised her hand to deliver a killing blow, but Sheni quickly grabbed her arm before she could take a swing.

"Fin tried to leave us for dead," he snapped. "I get why you had to kill her, maybe. But we can't murder our way out of every problem we come across!"

Gecki hissed in frustration and lowered her claws, but she kept her other hand pressed tight against the woman's chest.

"Which are you?" she barked, saliva spraying the inside of her visor. "Scavengers or Kilonova Corp?"

"Neither," the Kerulian replied, her terrified eyes flitting between the two of them. "Which are *you*?"

"Scavengers, I guess," Sheni said with as friendly a smile as possible, "but, you know, the good kind."

"Bunch of muloch crap," Gecki snarled. "If you ain't pirates or corporate, what the hell are you doing in the *Lucky Quark*?"

"Isn't it obvious?" she spluttered. "I live here. We all do."

Sheni and Gecki shared a panicked glance.

"*We?*" they asked in unison.

CHAPTER TWELVE

They followed the Kerulian through more abandoned corridors, always a few careful steps behind. A handful of cables and router boxes along the route were sparking, which meant at least *some* of the ship's generators were still operational.

"She's lying," Gecki muttered under her breath. "Another crew got here before us. She's leading us into a trap."

"Then why did the person on the other end of her radio tell her the noises she heard were just caused by vermin?" Sheni whispered. "If they broke in like us, they'd be on high alert. She isn't even armed. And it's not like we saw any other rovers parked outside the ship, is it?"

Gecki grumbled to herself, which was about as much a concession as Sheni was going to get.

"What's your name?" he asked their guide. "Did I hear your friend call you Lerrin?"

"Yeah, that's me. And who are you?"

"I'm Sheni. This here bundle of laughs is Gecki, and that's Alan. So, Lerrin. How'd you survive the crash?"

"How do you know I didn't drive out here through the storm and get stuck?"

Gecki growled. She already didn't trust Lerrin, and now the Kerulian was trying to avoid answering their questions.

"Nah, you're right," Lerrin said, sensing how close she was to having her oesophagus torn out. "I was on the *Lucky Quark* when she went down. Don't ask me what happened, coz I don't know. I *think* the captain wanted to skim the atmosphere, give the guests something cool to look at. Got too close to the storm and the whole ship got pulled in. But that's just what I heard. Captain's dead and I was in my room at the time."

"How the hell did you *survive*, though? We passed one of the ship's guards. They weren't so lucky."

"You found a body? Huh. I thought we'd got everyone. Not easy to reach every section of the ship, though. Most of us don't come down here much anymore."

Gecki bared her teeth and bunched her claws into fists.

"*Got* everyone?"

"Yeah," Lerrin replied, raising her feathery eyebrows. "Like, cleared all the bodies out. It's not all that hygienic, living in a graveyard. And to answer your question," she said, turning back to Sheni, "I was asleep in a cushioned bunk. Nothing hard to break my neck on, thank the stars. The ship fought against the storm the whole time, trying to launch itself back into orbit, so the impact wasn't as fast or hard as it could have been. Still enough to leave the *Quark* a lame wreck, though."

"Hasn't done you too much harm," Gecki said, relentless in her attempts to cast doubt on Lerrin's story. "You're still breathing after... how many years has it been? Three, three and a half? Long time to hold out on a dead ship. Surprised you never considered leaving."

"Only every damn day. We tried sending someone to get help, but they couldn't make it more than five minutes in that storm before they crawled back suffering from hypothermia. The only lifeboats on board are ships, not buggies, and they'd fare even worse in this atmosphere than the *Quark*. You're the first new faces we've seen since the crash."

"You keep saying 'we'," Sheni said. "How many other survivors are there?"

"A few. You'll see soon enough."

"I still don't like this," Gecki whispered. "Something feels off."

"Stop worrying so much," Sheni replied. "There are people on board the ship whether we like it or not. This way we'll know who and what we're dealing with, you know? Cards on the table, so to speak. Hey, maybe they'll even show us where all the credits are kept."

"Well, when you put it like that..."

Lerrin arrived at a wide industrial security door, the sort of emergency barrier that automatically cuts one sector of a ship off from another in the event of a crash. A crank wheel for manual release was set into a recess in its centre. Unlike the rest of the ship thus far, the lack of dust suggested somewhat regular use.

"I can't believe this is actually happening," she said, pausing to shake her head. "You promise you're not going to hurt anyone?"

"Scout's honour," Sheni replied, holding up his hand. "Gecki just got spooked when she heard you coming. Place is supposed to be deserted, you know? We came here looking for salvage, that's all. Figured there'd be plenty on a casino ship like this."

"All right. Fine." Lerrin reluctantly spun the wheel

crank. "I'm taking you to speak to Karrigan, so just follow me, okay? And don't take offence if people stare, or whatever. Like I said, nobody's made it to the *Quark* since we got here."

The door grunted open with a sound like a bowling ball crashing down a flight of concrete steps. Sheni shielded his eyes from the sudden brightness that burst through from the other side, then decided to remove his helmet. Clearly the air was fine to breathe, and whoever this Karrigan was, their conversation would probably fare better if it didn't sound like he was talking from the bottom of a fish bowl. He noticed Gecki unfastening hers, too. Alan had already hurried through.

"Stars above," Sheni mumbled as he followed the green meanie out onto a plush, carpeted balcony. "It's, erm, not quite what I expected."

They looked down at a marble-floored casino full of card tables and holographic chance games and plush benches flanked by convincing fake foliage. The majority of slot machines were still activated and jingling merrily away to themselves, though somebody had switched off the hall's ambient background music. The only other clue that the casino wasn't currently in official operation was the tatty nature of the velvety red curtains draping down the two-storey pillars. That, and the crystals missing from the central chandelier, which had presumably shaken loose in the crash. Even the defunct game machines had been swept clean of dust. Sheni counted at least three dozen people of various species crossing the floor, conversing, sometimes even sitting down to play the games. Three years of isolation hadn't done much to curb their addictions, it seemed.

"I mean, between the crashed *Quark* and the creaking

corridors of Borel-Six, I know which outpost I'd rather call home," he said, leaning against the railing.

"Lucky sods got trapped in paradise," Gecki rasped.

"Yes, well, that's the thing about paradises," Sheni replied, tapping the side of his head. "Once you're there, most don't let you leave."

"This way," Lerrin said, having sealed the security door behind them.

They followed her down a grand staircase lined with a smooth brass banister. As they descended, more and more of the *Lucky Quark's* residents noticed them, and soon an almighty cacophony of hushed mutterings consumed the casino hall. A crowd began to follow them as they made their way across to the reception area. It had been ridiculous to think they could pass through unnoticed, like the people here didn't have every single one of their neighbours' faces memorised.

Gecki tilted her head close to Sheni's and whispered, "Don't tell them anything important, all right? We don't know these people. They could have gone mad, stuck here with just the slot machines for company. Could have been mad to begin with! Let's keep *some* cards close to our chests, yeah?"

"You've got it."

"Did you really make it through the storm?" asked an Alpha Rhoden in crinkly evening wear who stomped alongside them. "What's it like out there? Are the Rhoden Rampagers still mudball champions?"

"You must take us with you," a desperate Oortilian in a sleek silver gown pleaded.

"Oh, no," Sheni replied with a dumb, friendly grin. "Our rover got torn to pieces just getting us here. We couldn't ferry anyone back to the outposts even if we had the room."

Gecki groaned and ran her claws down her face. So much for *that* potential bargaining chip.

Alan had been pottering across the casino floor with his button raised high above his head as if it were a winning lottery ticket. An elderly Luethian bent down to speak to him, her four hands pressed to her thighs.

"Aw, did somebody lose a button?" She pouted in exaggerated sympathy. "No problem, little one. We'll soon get that sewn back on."

"No, Alan, you should stay with..." Sheni tried to get Alan's attention, but it was no use. "And he's gone. Next time we see him, he'll be dealing out cards from behind a blackjack table."

"Or his skin will have been used to reupholster one," Gecki snarled. "I'm getting a bad feeling, Sheni. Everyone's too... normal. You know, in a weird way."

"I dunno, Gecki. If we ever spent three years in a place as swanky as this, I reckon we'd be pretty *normal*, too."

The crowd gradually dissipated as Sheni and Gecki climbed the short set of steps leading from the main casino floor to the *Lucky Quark's* reception. It had been repurposed into some kind of command centre. Arranged between the two rows of wood-panelled reception desks and a cluster of elevators whose chrome doors had lost their sheen was a nest of fold-out desks and crate stacks. Cables ran across the floor to hidden outlets like black jungle roots. An alligator-looking Krolak in *Lucky Quark* emblazoned power armour stood beside it, running through a checklist on his data pad.

"Karrigan," Lerrin said sharply. "I found these two lurking down near the disused generator rooms. Thought you should speak to them."

"Yes, Sylon just radioed ahead." Karrigan switched off

his data pad and eyed Sheni and Gecki with steely suspicion. "Thanks, Lerrin. I'll take it from here."

Lerrin nodded brusquely and then marched back down to the casino floor. Sheni thought he recognised Karrigan's voice from her walkie-talkie data pad, the one who thought they were just vermin scurrying about. He wondered if the guy's view of them had changed now they were face to face.

"You're not residents," Karrigan said, "so how the stars did you get here?"

"We drove," Gecki snarled. "Storm's in a lull phase. Only chance to make it through."

"Which means the company is probably on its way, too," the Krolak replied, visibly softening. "Thank the gods. We've been sending out a distress signal ever since we got the transmitter up and running again. Nothing's getting through, but we finally picked up a faint frequency yesterday. Must be the lull, like you said. Name's Karrigan, by the way. Head of Security for the *Quark*. Least I was before the ship went down. Now I just make sure nothing falls apart more than it already has. You've already met Lerrin. She's a kind of runner around here. Does whatever's needed, fills in for patrols, that sort of thing."

"Sheni Dupont," Sheni said, sticking out a hand for Karrigan to shake.

"Gecki." She settled for a curt nod. Even amongst other reptilians, it was less embarrassing to use her nickname than watch people attempt consonants meant for more dextrous tongues.

"How'd you end up at the *Quark*? You lost, or something?"

"We came here to claim salvage," Sheni said with an honest shrug. "The galaxy kind of assumes you're all dead."

Karrigan half-laughed, half-scoffed.

"Hopefully the company doesn't share that assumption. Thank you for being up front with me, though I hope we have an understanding that you won't strip my ship for parts. The *Lucky Quark* is still Kilonova property and, for the foreseeable future, our home. If Kilonova can't perform a rescue in the next few days, we'll likely be stuck here for another generation."

Sheni considered mentioning the giant Kilonova Corporation frigate floating in orbit almost directly above the *Lucky Quark's* coordinates, or the reports the company had filed that listed everybody on board as deceased, but decided to keep his mouth shut. That's what Gecki would want him to do, after all. They came here for credits. If he let slip that a rescue was imminent, they might start packing up everything valuable in the vault.

Besides, keeping Karrigan and his survivors in the dark a little while longer wouldn't do them any harm, would it? The Kilonova strike force would either get here in one piece, or they wouldn't, and there was nothing anyone on board the *Quark* could do about it.

"All that said," Karrigan continued, "the two of you must be exhausted, and I suspect there'll be a mob of residents hoping to ask you questions if you hang about much longer. I'll have a suite opened up for you. We've got plenty going spare. Come down whenever you feel like joining us. Just don't go wandering off by yourselves."

"Why, you got something to hide?" Gecki rasped with a tilt of her head. "Or don't you trust us?"

Karrigan snorted, waved over an insectoid in a weathered security uniform, and quickly relayed some instructions.

"If I'm totally honest," Karrigan continued, "no, I don't trust you. You're scavengers, by your own admission.

Thieves. But that's not why you need an escort. Sometimes it's easy to forget we live in a derelict ship. Not every sector of the *Quark* is as stable as the casino floor."

The security officer, whose faded name badge said Morton, used a keycard to unlock the elevators, then gestured inside the cabin as the dull chrome door hissed up into the ceiling.

"What was it the desk clerks used to say to guests?" Morton asked himself. "Oh yeah," he added, cracking a sarcastic smile. "Welcome to the *Lucky Quark*. We hope you have a pleasant stay."

CHAPTER THIRTEEN

Xotl adjusted the rags and rods with which they'd assembled their nest in the storage cubby. They didn't use it often, owing to their species' limited need for extended periods of sleep and Xotl's tendency to nap in their egg-cup pilot's seat whenever the *Silver Hart* was coasting through subspace, but it was nice to keep the place tidy. You never knew who might come visit.

Right. Another job ticked off the list. Back up to the cockpit they went.

Xotl knew they were a bit boring. Not uncharacteristically boring for their species – if anything, refusing the elders' call to return to Estroidea was quite daring, certainly enough so that Xotl was now exiled from their own homeworld. But boring compared to Gecki, or Sheni, or even Alan. They all disembarked the *Silver Hart* and had adventures. Often bad and dangerous and ill-fortuned adventures, but still. Xotl never left the ship.

They knew this wasn't their fault. The risk of catching a deadly infection was too great, even with the lovely custom enviro-suit the others had ordered for them. And normally they were fine being boring. In Xotl's line of work, boring meant things were going pretty good.

But what Xotl didn't appreciate quite as much was being *bored*.

They'd organised what remained of the ship's pantry. They'd chucked Sheni's dirty clothes in the laundry processor. They'd even checked in on the engine room to make sure nothing had fallen apart in Alan's absence, though they couldn't stay for long in case their ossicles dried out. Now that they'd arbitrarily rearranged the component parts of their nest, Xotl didn't think there was anything left to do but sit and wait.

Climbing up into their chair, Xotl gazed into the snowstorm blustering outside the cockpit windows with the dozens of tiny eyes scattered along their arms and around their beak. Their suckers dilated and contracted. The rest of the crew had been gone hours. By now, they should have reached the *Lucky Quark* and, with any luck, cracked open the vault. But it would still be the best part of another local rotation before they got back to the *Silver Hart*... presuming they got back at all.

What Xotl would do if the others died out there, they hadn't a clue. Not head back to Estroidea and beg the elders for forgiveness, that was for sure.

They wriggled up straight in their seat and stretched their arms as high as possible. Something had moved outside. And it wasn't the endlessly swirling blizzard. Nor was it just the groaning and croaking of the ship's hull making them freak out. *Something was out there*. A shadow stalking through the snow.

It couldn't be the crew. Not unless something went wrong early and they had to turn the rover around. But if that were the case, they would have opened comms once they were in range to say they were coming back...

There, just past the ship's nose. A lone figure stomping through the storm. Stars above, they were large. Looked strong enough to tear Xotl in half with their bare hands, if they wanted. Xotl desperately flapped their way over to the dashboard's remote airlock controls. Good. Still locked. Not that the security system would keep out somebody determined for long.

Xotl shivered. Who in the galaxy would be mad enough to approach the ship alone in this weather?

Patheer. Xotl dropped to the floor of the cockpit, beak-down with all five arms splayed out flat. Of course. Was it possible she had broken the rules and started her hunt early? Stars above. As if anything about her Prowlers' Rite was legal to begin with, loophole or no loophole. If she wanted to kick off her murder spree after just one day instead of one week, the stuck-up Felisian would do as she godsdamn pleased.

And she knew Gecki was the captain of the *Silver Hart*, didn't she? Must have tracked them to Gressil Prime. Probably thought Gecki and Sheni were holed up in the ship right this moment, hoping that the storm would hide them from her.

But they weren't. They were a hundred kilometres from here by now. All she would find was one frightened, defenceless Xocha, the pilot of the ship whose crew broke into her apartment. But a hunt was a hunt, and Xotl was sure Patheer would collect her blood however she could...

A heavy fist hammered the exterior airlock door. Xotl somehow managed to compress themself closer to the floor, trembling, wishing they'd give up and go away.

It didn't work. Another bout of thunderous knocks arrived ten seconds later.

"Hello?" they asked. "Excuse me?"

Xotl peeled a suckered arm off the floor. That voice sounded too low to belong to a Felisian. They nervously rose up to peer at the dashboard's grainy camera feed.

"Yes?" they spluttered into the intercom.

"Sorry to disturb ya," said Drairy, peering up at the camera from within the depths of an enormously furry overcoat, "but I couldn't help noticing your tail-wing's got a dent in it. Want me to buff that out for ya?"

CHAPTER FOURTEEN

Sheni collapsed onto the bed and waved his arms and legs about as if he were outside making snow angels. The component pieces of his enviro-suit lay scattered around the floor.

"You know what, Gecki? I'm sorry I doubted you. Breaking into the *Lucky Quark* was a stroke of genius."

His grumpy lizard companion snarled irritably as she stomped back and forth across the flamboyant suite. It reminded Sheni of a sultan's bedchamber. The walls were painted tasteful shades of yellow and blue. More drapes like those attached to the pillars of the casino floor flanked the wide, arching doorways. Soft light radiated from glow-orbs dangling from the high ceilings. The giant holo-screen occupying one wall of the lounge quarters was dead, and the suite's singular porthole offered a great view provided you enjoyed sheer walls of dark, icy rock, but he supposed it was only fair to overlook these shortcomings. The spacious bathroom had a jacuzzi, after all.

The *Lucky Quark* had been designed to accommodate the needs of guests from all corners of the galaxy, and the suite allocated to them was tailored to Kerulian tastes. The only major difference Sheni could find between this suite and one of the fancier Platinum-Tier condos on the human Ark ships was that the pillows here were stuffed with sponge instead of goose down. This wasn't surprising. Given the tufts of brightly coloured feathers that sprouted from Kerulians' temples, it would have been the equivalent of a human lying on a bed made of their own hair.

"I mean, look at this place! Have you ever seen anything like it? And the food." Sheni scooted to the edge of the bed and plucked a synthetic drumstick from the spread laid out for them on the waxed wooden coffee table. "Don't tell me this isn't better than anything you'd get at a Xondo's."

Gecki responded only with another distracted grunt. She scratched erratically at the flaky scales beneath her chin. Sheni shrugged and tucked into his drumstick. He'd lined up a steaming bowl of noodles and an intricately iced Bursaagu pastry for after. He was halfway through chewing the mysterious meat when inspiration struck.

"Stars above, I've just had a thought. We could stay here forever, you know? It's not like we could ever afford a life like this outside the *Quark*. And Patheer would never find us, not with the storm blocking ships from flying through the Gellar Valley. Alan would be happy, too. Think of all the old engine rooms he could explore. Probably get half of them up and running again, knowing him."

Gecki finally stopped pacing. She glared at Sheni and spread her clawed hands out wide in exasperation.

"And what about Xotl, Sheni?"

Sheni tore another bite out of his drumstick as he considered this.

"All right, that would suck a bit. I'd miss the floppy freak.

But they'd be fine, wouldn't they? Xotl spends all their time in the *Silver Hart* as it is."

"Until Patheer and her furry goons track the ship to Gressil Prime and pull the poor starfish out the airlock, you idiot."

"Pfft. As far as Patheer knows, Xotl had nothing to do with us breaking into her apartment."

"You think Patheer cares? She knows the *Silver Hart* dropped us off outside her window. If she can't get her blood from us, you can bet your mammalian hide Xotl will pay the price instead."

Sheni slumped back onto the bedsheets having momentarily lost his appetite.

"Yeah, I suppose you're right. And we won't be able to stay here for very long, anyway. That Kilonova strike force will be here soon enough, and then the party's over."

"I hardly think this is a party, Sheni. What's luxurious and decadent for you is a prison for everyone stuck here. These people have friends and family out in the real world. People who think they're dead, who may even have moved on without them. And these are just the lucky few who survived the crash."

Sheni dumped the rest of the drumstick in the trash and skipped straight to his dessert.

"Then I'm glad there's someone here who appreciates how freakin' awesome this grub is, you know?" he said through a mouthful of pastry. "Especially when that someone is me."

Gecki shook her head and hissed.

"I should have known you wouldn't take this seriously. The whole drive you were complaining and panicking and telling me we should turn back. Now you're here, you're content to just stuff your face and sink into the furniture."

"I mean, yeah? That's why we scavenge and steal, right? So one day we can live like this. So we can do whatever we want without worrying where our next meal's coming from. Like hell I'm not gonna enjoy this while I can."

"You're so short sighted! What's one nice spread compared to a lifetime of banquets? We should be cracking open that vault right now, before Kilonova shows up and takes the lot."

Sheni struggled to swallow, ended up coughing from the dry pastry flakes going the wrong way down his throat.

"You still want to steal the casino's credit reserves? Even with all the guests and security guards here?"

"Absolutely! So what if there are a few more potential witnesses than we anticipated? It's worth the risk. What are they gonna do if they catch us, anyway?"

"Force us to march back out into the storm," Sheni suggested.

"Argh, don't be stupid." Gecki waved away his concern. "They wouldn't get the chance, not with Kilonova on the way. And that's another good thing about having all these people here. When the company discovers they're missing a tonne of credits, they've got plenty of suspects to pin the blame on."

"Something tells me Kilonova will point their finger at the trio of scavengers who showed up at the last minute over the poor, unfortunate custodians who went years without stealing so much as a single credit. Presumably," he quickly added. "We don't even know if that vault's got anything left in it. The survivors could be using the credits to trade amongst themselves. Or they might have wired all the digital currency to their own data pads in anticipation of getting rescued!"

"Nah, I don't see Karrigan allowing everyone on board to

help themselves to whatever they want from the vault, do you? I reckon its doors haven't been opened since the crash. And what's more, I bet it's not even guarded. Everyone trying to survive on board this gaudy madhouse has much better things to do."

"I dunno, Gecki. It's one thing to steal from the Kilonova Corporation, and another thing altogether to pinch stuff from under the residents' noses. We agreed to only target those who don't deserve what they've got, remember? I mean, what if we explained our situation to the people here, ask them for a couple hundred thousand credits? I'm sure they wouldn't mind. Or we could see what we can scavenge from the sectors they haven't managed to bring online. I bet there's a tonne of good salvage Karrigan and his crew won't miss from this ship, especially if they might be leaving soon."

"And how are we supposed to smuggle a class B drive core out of here, huh? Even if we somehow got the rover up and running again, there's no way we could use it to haul back two hundred thousand credits' worth of junk and spare parts. Face it, Sheni. We either get inside that vault, or we head home empty handed."

"If we head home at all," he reminded her, clapping his hands clean of crumbs. "Like you said, the rover ain't operational, and there's no guarantee that Kilonova squad will make it through the storm. Sorry, Gecki. I'm not accepting these people's hospitality and then going behind their backs like that. It just doesn't feel right, you know?"

"Having your entrails batted about the room by Patheer won't feel right either, godsdammit!" Gecki snarled and stomped off toward the suite's front door. "Whatever. Sit there and get fat. I'll go fix our problems, *as per usual.*"

She stormed out. Probably would have slammed the

door if it weren't run on hydraulics. Sheni sat at the foot of the bed and shrugged to himself. So what if he *did* get fat? Back in the Middle Ages, being on the plump side was a good thing. Meant you could afford to feed yourself. Stars, he *wished* the girth of his waistband was the sort of problem he had the privilege to worry about.

But he was already quite stuffed, and even the idea of nibbling another drumstick made him feel a bit queasy. Gecki didn't know how to enjoy a good thing, did she? Sheni had his doubts she could ever be content, not even if she left the *Quark* with every penny the casino coveted. But there was grumpy, and there was being one poorly worded remark away from literally biting someone's head off. Something was eating away at Gecki worse than usual. Worse than the way he'd just eaten through this spread...

He burped, covered his mouth and composed himself.

As tempting as it was to simmer in the jacuzzi and then wriggle about under the bed's satin sheets like a bloated python, Gecki was right about one thing. He was wasting his time sitting in this suite, stuffing his mouth.

There was a whole freakin' resort to explore.

CHAPTER FIFTEEN

After navigating the fancy carpeted corridors of the residential suites and riding the elevator back down to the reception lobby, Sheni found himself in possession of a chaperone.

Lerrin was considerably less excited about the grand tour than he was. But Karrigan had specifically requested that she do it given she was one of the few survivors of the *Lucky Quark* unlikely to bombard Sheni with inane questions, and it wasn't like she had anything better to be getting on with. You know, like making sure rodents didn't chew through the generator cables and leave everyone without heating.

They descended onto the bustling casino floor. Fortunately, without his enviro-suit, Sheni was a little less conspicuous.

"Is there a reason why all the games are still online?" he asked, just trying to make conversation.

"Not really," Lerrin replied, shrugging. "The slot machines all belong to the same main breaker as the lights and air recyclers. I'm sure we could switch each of them off individually, but there's not much point. And I reckon a casino without games would make everyone even more depressed than they are already."

They passed a bejewelled octopod who was repeatedly pulling the lever of a one-armed bandit, a tired and faraway look in their horizontally-slitted eyes.

"Oh, yeah," Sheni replied dubiously. "They really liven up the place."

The casino floor seemed to stretch on forever. Sheni couldn't imagine how many people used to frequent it from day to day as the *Quark* slowly migrated from one star system to the next. They hadn't been anywhere near to full capacity when they crashed into Gressil Prime, thank goodness. The two of them encountered endless carousels of excitable fruit machines, all practically indistinguishable from each other but extremely different in their experiences, according to Lerrin; weird cylindrical booths in which holographic die bounced about; card tables which, more often than not, were covered in toolkits and empty bottles rather than cards and credit chips; long booths with randomised laser displays; sunken pits in which virtual creatures could beat the digital crap out of one another; arcade games; and, of course, bars with enormous screens where drunken patrons could bet on mudball matches and hover-bike races being broadcasted from every corner of the galaxy.

In theory, Sheni loved it. But he knew a money-trap when he saw one. Even if he had every credit on board the *Quark* in his pocket, it would only take a few days before his entire fortune ended up back in the casino's vault.

"So, you said you were a guest here. Must have a pretty fancy life you want to get back to, right?"

Lerrin laughed like he'd said something funny.

"Stars, I wish. Nah, I just came for the experience. We've all got the same sort of suites now, of course. No point in having a hierarchy when there's so many apartments going spare. But when I signed up for the cruise, I could only afford one of the tiny coffin bunks. Which was fine. I just needed a place to sleep. The package I chose, you prepaid for board and lodging. That way, even if you lost the rest of your credits at the roulette tables – which, of course, everyone does sooner or later – you wouldn't go hungry for the remainder of your trip. I was having a pretty good time until the crash. Better than what I'd have back home, anyway."

"Huh. Well, it sure seems like you got your money's worth from this place."

"I know, right? I don't think the company quite anticipated how many free meals they'd owe me when I signed up for the week. Hey, through here."

Lerrin guided him under a wide archway whose upper half was blocked by an industrial security shutter. It had presumably come crashing down during the impact, but the survivors had managed to wrench it most of the way open again. They emerged in a long, comparatively narrow promenade lined with what looked like expensive storefronts. Most of them were shuttered or had suffered cave-ins. Sheni spotted the lifeless facade of a Xondo's burger joint, its windows smashed and holographic menu perpetually glitching. Some of the girders in the ceiling had collapsed and sections of the hull – or the interior bulkhead, at the very least – had been welded back together with patches of scrap metal salvaged from elsewhere in the ship. A few residents of the *Quark* crossed the mall carrying sacks and boxes.

"What is this place?" Sheni asked.

"The land where all our free food comes from," Lerrin replied with a dry wink. "There used to be almost twenty restaurants and fast food outlets here, but obviously we didn't bother getting the takeaway stuff operational again. Nobody around to man the stations. Made more sense to pool together all the ingredients that survived the crash and use just a few of the kitchens."

Peering inside the closest restaurant's massive, open plan set-up, Sheni saw a female Bursaag stirring a large iron pot on an extremely complicated stove. The tusked, bear-like chef raised a massive paw and gave them both a polite wave. Sheni waved back.

"That's Bena Ursula," Lerrin said. "She does the most *amazing* desserts. You got a dinner basket in your suite, right? Half of it was probably baked by her."

They followed the food court toward the bow of the ship. A question bugged Sheni as they passed the derelict Xondo's.

"How many people were on board the *Lucky Quark* when it went down, do you know?"

"Erm, close to two thousand, I think. Including crew."

"And how many live here now?"

"Three hundred and sixteen. That's actually a couple more than when we crashed. There's been a few babies since."

"People are having kids here?"

Lerrin shrugged. "I mean, there's not a huge lot for people to do..."

"So, three hundred plus people times three and a half years. That's a hell of a lot of meals to make. Where are you getting all the food from?"

"Well, the *Quark* was stocked to feed many thousands

more people than were on board at the time of the crash. And, of course, barely fifteen percent of passengers and crew survived. That's quite the surplus. And we grow some of our own food, too. Karrigan set up a hydroponic lab in the old steam chambers. But the replicator can synthesise most ingredients we need now it's hooked up to the waste recyclers."

"Waste recyclers?" Sheni's stomach performed a somersault – quite the acrobatic feat for an organ so full. "You don't mean...?"

"Yeah, my advice is not to think about it too much. Ruins your appetite. Oh, look. Your friend's back."

Sheni spun around expecting to find Gecki lurking behind him, vault-cracking toolkit in hand, but nobody was there. Then he looked down. Alan stared past both of Sheni's shoulders, his gormless smile poking up from the collar of a coat that finally had all its buttons in the right place. The little guy was holding a sugary stick that resembled a churro.

"Ah, Alan. Good to see you again. I'm glad nobody's turned you into a lampshade."

"What?" Lerrin asked, an eyebrow raised.

"Nothing." Sheni bent down to speak to his tiny crewmate. "Are you joining us for the tour, Alan? If you're well behaved, maybe we can see if there's—"

Alan turned and pottered off down a nearby connecting corridor.

"Don't take it personally," Sheni said to Lerrin. "I don't think there's much that can hold his attention for long. What's in that direction?"

"Erm, not a lot. Security, I think, though given Karrigan's taken on more of an administrative role these days and half the security systems aren't even online anymore, there's not a lot to find there. And past that is the bridge. That sector's off-limits, though."

"Why's that?"

"Too dangerous. Floor's unstable and one of the emergency generators up there went into overdrive, spitting sparks all over the place. Big leak, too, just to make matters worse. There's nothing anyone needs up there, though, so whatever. Hey, you like sims?"

"What, like virtual reality stuff?" Sheni followed Lerrin through a crank-sealed hatch at the far end of the food court. "Yeah, it's all right. Headsets make me feel a bit nauseous, though, you know? Like someone's put my head in a vice."

"Haven't used a headset since I was a kid," she replied, smirking. "The salon here had sim-rigs like you wouldn't *believe*. Full haptic feedback. Huge catalogue of software to choose from. Private and social booths. Proper next-level stuff."

"Sounds great. Is it still up and running?"

"Nah." She sealed the hatch shut behind them. "Got annihilated in the crash. Even totalled the servers, so we couldn't transfer the sims to our data pads, or whatever. Really sucks, because a way to escape the *Quark* is exactly what everyone's needed since."

Lerrin pulled a lever beside the hatch. Dim lights clunked on in sequence from their side of the hall all the way to its far end. Before them sprawled a small town of theatres, galleries, carnival attractions and glitzy arcades, all styled to resemble sleek, icy-blue Oortilian architecture. It even boasted a roller coaster that wound a looping, corkscrewing and now, thanks to the stretch of broken track, quite fatal path around the sector's perimeter. It looked like a bomb had decimated about a third of the district. The few panels on the ceiling that weren't completely ruined flickered on to reveal a live feed of the swirling grey storm outside. Under normal circumstances, they would have shown the stars.

"Woah," was all Sheni managed to say.

"Boy, this place used to be something." Lerrin crossed her arms and shook her feathered head. "Variety shows, big spinners, a zero-g playground for the children. There was even a gallery of Kwoo Fim wood carvings, can you believe it? Got reduced to matchsticks when we hit the ground. Pretty sure people used what was left as firewood before we got the heaters working again, actually..."

Sheni continued to marvel at the ship's entertainment centre. It reminded him of the amusement parks back on Earth, the ones that had closed their doors long before the Arks left for the stars. He'd been born a few years too late to visit one.

"Does *anything* in this place still work?" he asked hopefully.

"The rides, no." Lerrin grimaced. Sheni's heart fell. "Most of the performers are dead, obviously, and I think you're a bit too big for the playground. But the holotheatre... we got the projectors working a year or two back. Can't say how well they're still holding up, but I suppose we could give it a go?"

She shrugged apologetically. To her surprise, Sheni clapped his hands together in glee.

"All right, then," he said, breaking into a huge grin. "Let's see if there ain't some fun to be squeezed from the *Lucky Quark* yet."

CHAPTER SIXTEEN

While Sheni was trying to briefly restore one old girl to her former glory, Gecki was determined to do the same.

The sight of a grumpy Eureptix stomping down the corridors of the residential deck in full enviro-suit get-up was enough to prevent any survivor of the *Lucky Quark* from stopping her to ask questions about politics or the stock market. She wasn't headed back down to the lobby with the reception desks. If Karrigan caught sight of her, he'd make sure a chaperone stuck to her side like a limpet. Or worse – she'd be forced to take a tour of the ship with that idiot, Sheni.

Stupid humans. So easily distracted. Had he forgotten why they drove through a deadly storm to get here in the first place? What kind of life awaited them if they could only get into the ship's vault?

Ah, whatever. She didn't need him. She didn't even need a crew, not once she had millions of credits to her name. Maybe she'd throw him a few thousand, just out of charity, before setting off for tropical shores on her own.

Gecki stumbled across an elevator on the far side of the residential deck and prodded a button for the deck below. The cabin grumbled and shook as it descended. She bared her teeth in a snarl. It was easy to forget she was on board a derelict ship. Not everything that was technically operational was actually still safe to use.

Gods, she wished she could shake this damn suit off. But she needed the tools stashed inside its various pockets and compartments. Without clothes, she wouldn't even have somewhere to put all the stolen credit chips.

The elevator door opened onto the casino floor, and she was greeted by a wave of ear-achingly trite jingles. She was well out of sight of Karrigan and his security goons, though. Good. She quickly skulked through the low-clearance archway to her left.

She found herself in a commercial promenade lined with shops. A fashion boutique here, a CyberSplice showroom there. All of the lights were off, the shutters often down, the shelves looted and bare. A gangly Garnidian had set up a desk in one of the stores, but it didn't look like they were selling anything, only using it as a quiet place to work away from all the mechanical melodies. They looked up at Gecki as she passed, and Gecki returned as friendly a smile as she could muster. Perhaps her smile was a little on the toothy side, because the Garnidian quickly returned her gaze to the schematics on her desk.

Three quarters of the way down the promenade, Gecki came across a connecting corridor on her left. She stopped and studied the wonky, slightly charred sign hanging above it.

"Security," she read aloud. "Yeah, that'll do."

The short corridor was hexagonal, clinical, a grey sort of off-white colour. Definitely not public-facing, even before one of the pipes in the floor had burst. A staircase to Gecki's right led up to the Security division and down, she suspected, to another section of the engineering deck, but movement past the other end of the corridor momentarily caught her attention.

She stalked towards the promenade opposite, careful not to be seen, taking quick sniffs of the air. Hmm. Food. *Sugary* food. Her stomach rolled. Maybe she shouldn't have shunned that dinner basket after all...

Poking her snout around the corner, she hurriedly jerked her head back behind the doorframe. Sheni was standing by the restaurants talking to that Lerrin woman, the one Gecki had almost eviscerated down near the engine rooms. They looked all chummy together, like they were neighbours or something, like Sheni had been living on the crashed ship for years. What a fool. One moment's luxury and he was acting like the *Quark* wasn't one rusty bolt away from collapsing around their aural canals.

Alan was with them, too. He looked like he was threatening them with some kind of doughy baton, maybe? Then suddenly he was waddling across the avenue of eateries, right in her direction...

She flattened herself against the wall of the corridor. The bobble-hatted loon bumbled right past her. Gecki grabbed hold of his coat before he could disappear down into the bowels of the ship.

"Oh no you don't. I need your help with something."

Alan blinked at her blankly, waggled his churro, and then followed her up the stairs.

The *Lucky Quark's* Security division was as sterile and high-tech as Gecki expected of a ship designed to accommodate extremely wealthy (and therefore infinitely targetable) clientele. The unmanned desk to her right as they reached the top of the stairwell possessed a computer that looked as advanced as the quantum processors calculating the probability of the slot machines below, and past that was a huge ring of forcefield projectors that could completely seal the division off from unwanted visitors. Fortunately, they were deactivated, along with any rotary cannons and tranquilliser turrets no doubt concealed within the innocently plastic walls.

Still, Gecki stepped carefully, peering around every cubicle in search of dormant security guards. The offices were deserted, as she expected. The security cameras weren't online, either. Or if they were, the feeds were being rerouted to monitors elsewhere in the ship. There were still a few battle rifles locked away in black and yellow striped gun cases mounted on the walls, though – secured with physical padlocks *and* digital keypads that probably wouldn't even work unless certain electrical subsystems got reactivated.

Alan stood facing a tall, glass-fronted cabinet, chewing his churro. Inside was a chunky security-bot. Gecki rapped a cautious knuckle against the transparent window of its case. No response. The unit was completely powered down.

"Sleep tight, bolt bucket," she rasped. "Ignore it, Alan. We've got a job to do."

She salivated as they pushed through the deactivated security scanners in the next room. There it was, the vault. A big black square of a door surrounded by valved pistons, bolts and chromium hinges. Rather frustratingly, it was probably the only part of the ship sturdy enough to remain entirely intact despite the crash. A pair of overturned carts, used to transfer lockboxes full of credits up to the safe from the casino floor before the *Quark* fell out of the sky, lay with their wheels pointing up at the ceiling. Another fancy computer terminal that looked like a mixing deck was built into the desk installed perpendicular to the vault door.

Gecki tapped its buttons and triggers, but the screen in the centre of the deck remained blank. Godsdammit. The computer was as dead as everything else around there.

"Try to get this computer online, will you?" she asked Alan. "I'll see what the door's got in store for us."

She ran her gloves over the surface of the vault. Tungsten. The plasma torch could cut through its layers, maybe, but it would take a hell of a long time. And that was presuming there was enough fuel in its canister. A drill would have definitely been better, but it would have been noisier, too. The next question was, which parts of the door to cut? A small hole in the centre *might* be easiest. Simply slicing through the pistons might be quicker, but it also might render the door shut for good. Then again, there were probably all sorts of electronic countermeasures in place for that exact eventuality, especially with the primary power source offline.

Decisions, decisions...

When she glanced back over at Alan, he was exactly where she left him.

"Why are you just standing there?" she snarled. "For once in your life, I *want* you to fiddle about with things!"

Alan dribbled slightly.

"Come on, you braindead loon. Think of all the spare buttons and hessian sacks and pet woodlice a million credits could buy you!"

Alan blinked.

"I'll... I'll get you your own ship to work on. Nothing

fancy, mind you, just a junker, but you can break it down and fix it up however you like!"

Without either of his eyes swivelling so much as an inch, Alan shoved the frayed ends of two wires together. The computer bleeped and whirred back to life.

"That's the spirit," Gecki said with a triumphant grin. "You drive a hard bargain, Alan. I can respect that. Now, all we need to do is convince the system to open the door..."

She hit a key to wake the screen. Even after rebooting its power source, the computer wouldn't so much as bring up the Kilonova logo without a corporate password. This was hardly unexpected. It was a giant safe, after all. You couldn't just politely ask your way inside.

"Okay, fine, we'll do it the hard way." She retrieved her black market data drive from the pocket opposite her plasma torch and plugged it into one of the terminal's ports. "You'd better not have sold me cruddy tech, Peggi..."

The data drive set out restoring the terminal to its factory settings. It wouldn't open the door necessarily, but it might give her access to the sub-routines which could. At the very least, it would ensure they didn't encounter any nasty booby-traps if and when they cut their way through with the torch.

A little over a minute later, the desk made an unhealthy high-pitched noise. The screen turned a strange blue colour. Safe Mode. Gecki grinned and navigated the simplified directories until she found the one that kept the door sealed. She pressed a key and a harsh hissing sound burst out from around the vault door. One by one, the bolts shot back into their holes and the pistons sighed in defeat.

Until one didn't.

"No, you piece of..." Gecki frantically tried to restart the sequence. "Don't do this to me!"

Alan waddled off into the security offices. When he returned he was carrying the metal leg of someone's chair. He proceeded to absolutely batter the piston with it.

"Are you crazy?" Gecki rasped, wincing at the sharp din. "Someone will hear..."

The last piston suddenly relaxed into position. The vault door slowly grumbled open. Inside lay shelf upon shelf of credits and lockboxes and the odd jewellery case, all glittering under the safe's soft interior lights like they were made of crystal and gold.

"Yes!" Gecki snarled, grabbing Alan by the coat and screaming into his gormless face. "You beautiful weirdo, I knew we could do it! Grab everything you can get your claws on. Quickly!"

Alan doddered inside in search of individual coins to pocket while Gecki got to work brushing all of the credit chips and data drives off the shelves and into the various compartments of her enviro-suit. There had to be tens of thousands of credits on her person already, and they hadn't even got to the blinking terminal at the back that housed all of the digital reserves that should have been automatically transferred off-ship during the crash, but weren't. She was already rich. But soon... soon she'd be *wealthy*.

She was just about to link her data pad up to the terminal and transfer across a large fortune when she realised she was totally alone in the vault.

"Alan?" she hissed. "*Alan!* Where in the stars have you got to?"

Behind her, she heard the dull click of a rifle's safety catch being thumbed off.

"Hands behind your head, scavenger."

Gecki did as instructed and slowly turned around. Karrigan stood in the doorway of the vault with his rifle trained on her skull. His insectoid buddy Morton lurked and smirked a few metres further back with a rifle of his own. Gecki growled impatiently.

"Don't be stupid," she rasped. "We could all be rich."

"Not if we're dead, we won't be." Karrigan shook his head. "Kilonova's the only way off this planet, and this vault's our ticket out of here."

CHAPTER SEVENTEEN

He took some persuading, but Karrigan finally relented and allowed Sheni to visit Gecki in her cell. Another one of his security officers, a grey and chiseled Drygg, had been tasked with accompanying Sheni at all times, however.

He was escorted to another sector of the Security division, one located as far from the vault as logistically possible. There were only three cells. Gecki had been locked inside the one at the far end. She was trapped behind a red-tinted forcefield. To make matters worse, they'd had to reroute power from some of the lights in the food court to get the cell's forcefield working. According to Lerrin, they hadn't had cause to use the cells since the crash, when a few of the survivors had gone a little stir crazy.

The Drygg stopped beside the doorway to the holding cells with her back to the wall. Sheni pressed a button beside Gecki's soundproof cell to activate the comms. She twisted around to face him with a start.

"Proud of ourselves, are we?" he said.

Gecki shooed him away with a wave of her claws.

"I was so close, Sheni. Thousands of credits in my suit, one cable away from transferring a lifetime's credits to my data pad. If you'd been there to help, we'd both be millionaires by now."

"Nah, Gecki. We'd both be in that cell instead. I told you stealing from a populated ship was a dumb idea, didn't I?"

"It wasn't dumb, you idiot. It was daring. We'll never captain our own fleet if we don't take risks."

"Why is having a fleet so important?"

"Because Patheer is on the prowl," Gecki snarled, jumping up from her modest bench and approaching the forcefield, "and she'll kill us if we don't cough up two hundred thousand credits. Because if we were rich, nobody would mess with us, and we'd finally be free from all these debts and desperate schemes. We wouldn't just be a bunch of misfits floating from one stupid idea to the next anymore. We'd be... I dunno. Remembered, maybe."

She'd lost her gusto by the time she finished. With another dismissive wave of her claws, she collapsed back onto her bench and began stripping off the component pieces of her enviro-suit.

"What's been bothering you the past few weeks?" Sheni asked. "The Gecki I know couldn't give two shakes of a scale what anyone else thinks of her. And she'd never suggest robbing a casino that's still got people in it, you know? Probably would have spaced me out an airlock if *I'd* come up with the idea. Is this because of The Change?"

Gecki rolled her head in exasperation.

"Will you and Xotl shut up about "The Change"? What the hell do you and a godsdamn starfish know about Eureptix biology, anyway?"

Sheni raised an eyebrow.

"Is that a yes...?"

"Gods! No!" Gecki growled irritably. "You'll be dribbling on your zimmer frame before I start showing any signs of" – she shuddered – "*masculinity*. Stars above, you'd think your species had never heard of sequential hermaphroditism before."

"What is it, then?"

"I've been a pirate or a raider for as long as you've been alive, human. First, when I was barely more than a male hatchling, I ran with other crews. Did what their captains told me to do. Always hungry for the next job, like I was making a name for myself. Squirrelled away enough credits to buy my own ship. Only a one-seater. Pulled more jobs, upgraded the ship. Eventually stole the *Silver Hart* and assembled my own crew. But I'm still just scraping by. Forty cycles of hustling and fighting tooth and claw, and nothing's really changed, has it?"

"Hey, I dunno. Like you said, you've got your own crew. That's pretty neat. And think of all the heists we've pulled off over the years. It's not nothing, right?"

"Nobody's ever heard of the jobs we've done," she rasped. "Not really. And even those who have certainly don't believe *we're* the ones who pulled them off. We're small fry. Nobody knows our names."

"You want to be famous?" Sheni grimaced. "That's not a healthy trait for a pirate. Sort of limits your career prospects."

"Not famous," Gecki replied, rolling her yellow eye. "*Infamous*. Like, people would hear the name *Silver Hart* and think twice about crossing us. Or at least say to themselves, woah, they're the guys who plundered the *Lucky Quark*, or whatever. But we're just a laughing stock. There's nothing special about us. We're just like every other crew drinking their lives away in the Corpse & Casket."

Sheni said nothing. He *wanted* to say, "And what's wrong with that?" but he'd seen what a lifetime of drunken mediocrity did to old-timers like Guntho and Ole Nana Sue.

"I just thought I'd have achieved something big by now, that's all," Gecki continued with a sigh. "That reckless little hatchling set some pretty lofty goals for himself. I figured robbing the *Quark* was my last chance to prove him – prove *me* – right."

"Nah, don't be like that, Gecki. There'll be plenty more heists to come!"

"I dunno, Sheni. I might be nowhere near The Change," she said pointedly, "but I'm way past my prime. If this captain was gonna achieve notoriety, it would have happened already."

Sheni slumped to the floor on the other side of the forcefield.

"I don't know if being rich and famous – sorry, *infamous* – would make you happy. There's always a bigger score, right? And a bigger crew, or a fleet, or whatever – it comes with a whole new set of problems, you know? But enough credits to keep ourselves fed, to stay out of the sights of people like Slugbarrow and Patheer... *that* I can understand. We do seem to keep running into the same problems, like we're going round in a big circle."

"Like when I try driving a rover in a blizzard, you mean," Gecki said, smiling slightly.

"Exactly." Sheni rapped his knuckles against the flickering hard light behind his back. "Now, let's work the problem, as you say. How are we gonna convince Karrigan to let you out of there?"

Remembering the guard Karrigan had tasked with being his chaperone, Sheni glanced back to the doorway of the holding cells. But the security officer was gone. An ominous light was blinking on the inter-divisional comm unit installed in the wall where they'd stood.

"That's... pretty weird," he said, climbing to his feet. "I'll be right back."

"Sure," Gecki replied, scratching her scales. "Take your time..."

Sheni cautiously poked his head out of the door. The entire security office was deserted, even the room housing the methodically re-locked vault. He descended the steps to the connecting corridor and ventured into the promenade housing all of the defunct restaurants. A few well-dressed guests hurried past him towards the casino floor.

"Where's everyone going?" he shouted after them.

"It's the Kilonova Corporation," the excited resident replied. "They're here."

CHAPTER EIGHTEEN

Everyone gathered as close to the reception lobby as Karrigan's fellow security officers would allow, which meant a great deal of the *Lucky Quark's* population were crowded around – and in a few cases on – the casino's slot machines and card tables. After years spent stranded in an inescapable storm, nobody wanted to miss the moment when rescue finally arrived.

Sheni was probably the only one amongst them not feeling some sense of relief. He didn't really care that the Kilonova Corporation was here to reclaim their lost credits. The crew of the *Silver Hart* would find another way to get Patheer's hunt called off. Everything always worked out fine in the end. But Gecki was still locked up in her cell. When Kilonova found out why she'd been apprehended... well, there went any chance of him, Gecki and Alan blagging a ride back home.

Which meant they'd be stuck here, just like the survivors of the *Lucky Quark* had been. Only this time, rescue wouldn't come for another fifteen years... if it ever came at all. Because there's not much point in risking life and limb driving out to a wreckage whose treasures have already been plundered, is there?

And from the tour Lerrin had given him, Sheni suspected the Kilonova Corporation had arrived just in the nick of time. Sure, the survivors had done wonders getting parts of the ship operational again. And they lived in relative luxury, provided they stuck to the same few sectors. But even with regular upkeep, Sheni couldn't imagine the ship holding itself together for more than another year or two.

Up by his makeshift command centre between the reception desks, past the excited and apprehensive crowds, Karrigan waited for the doors at the far end of the lobby to open. From what one of his scouts had told him – and this was just what Sheni had heard being whispered by the gossiping residents – the strike force had entered via the guests' shuttle bay, a sector the survivors had deemed inaccessible. Karrigan wanted the lobby as clear as possible so that when they finally cut through its Herculean security door, nobody on either side was taken too much by surprise.

Think, Sheni. Think. He wracked his brains for a solution out of this mess. Maybe stealing the credits with Gecki would have been the smart move. He could try again while everyone was distracted. Now was the perfect time, if he was quick. But he didn't have Gecki's tools. And even if Alan – wherever he was – helped him get it open a second time, and they downloaded every credit off the vault's computer, what about Gecki? She was still stuck inside that cell, and no way was he good enough at hacking security systems to switch that forcefield off.

Okay, skip that step. Presume you *can* get Gecki free, and

the three of you try and escape with or without the *Quark's* loot. You're still trapped on board this casino without a set of working wheels. And if you do have the *Quark's* loot, you can bet your ass that Kilonova will figure out the vault's been robbed before they start shipping survivors back to the outposts. So your only option, Sheni, is to steal one of the strike force's trucks. The ones which are probably locked and definitely owned by people with big guns.

But even if you can steal one, and you manage to drive all the way back to Borel-Six and fly away in the *Silver Hart*... how many Kilonova goons or *Lucky Quark* survivors will be left behind, effectively sentenced to death, given the unexpected shortage of vehicles?

Sheni groaned. He couldn't see a way out of this. Maybe if he freed Gecki, and if he somehow convinced Karrigan not to mention anything about her attempted heist to Kilonova... maybe they could hitch a ride back with everyone else.

Maybe.

But even if he looked at every outcome in the most positive of lights... this whole situation still felt wrong.

And he reckoned it had something to do with the Kilonova Corporation having no more idea there were three hundred and sixteen survivors on board the *Lucky Quark* than Sheni had before he arrived.

"Capricious variables," gurgled a small voice down by his left foot.

"Oh, hello, Alan. Yeah, this is a real sticky situation we've got ourselves into, you know?"

The security door hissed and sparked as somebody on the other side cut through it with a plasma torch that likely put Gecki's pocket-sized tool to shame. Everybody on the casino floor hushed. This was it. They were finally getting off this wreck and back to their fancy Kapamentis penthouses, their moon condos, the oak-panelled offices of their trans-stellar businesses. Presuming they still owned the deeds to them, that is, and they hadn't been passed on to their next of kin. The galaxy thought they were dead, after all.

Alan tugged on Sheni's hand.

"What is it, little guy?"

Alan continued to yank Sheni towards the rear of the casino. The gormless grape was still smiling underneath his plump jacket, but there was a sincere and determined look in his normally vacuous eyes. Sheni sighed and relented.

"Fine, but you'd better be taking me somewhere with a good view. Show's about to start."

He followed Alan halfway down the hall through the throng of expectant faces to a raised platform beside the roulette stands. The crowd grew sparse there, more so the closer Kilonova's arrival drew. Sheni climbed up and squeezed in beside a slender Oortilian.

"I'm not sure this is much of an improvement," he said, squinting and scrunching his nose. "Karrigan's barely more than a speck from here."

Alan wriggled in Sheni's grasp and tried to pull them deeper into the casino ship. Looking for an engine to break, most probably. Sheni kept a tight grip on his hand. Whatever happened with Kilonova, whether they could get Gecki out of that jail cell or not, they needed to stick together.

"No, Alan, I want to see. We need to figure out what we're doing next, you know?"

The hissing – barely the whisper of wind blowing through reeds from Sheni's new vantage point – stopped and the flashing sparks disappeared. With a lethargic, mechanical grunt, the security doors rumbled apart. Everybody in the casino stiffened and fell totally silent.

The wide connecting corridor linking the resort and the shuttle bay was pitch black, its lights off, the electrical systems terminally offline. Motes of stale dust billowed in from the abandoned sector. And then, with a gasp from their audience, figures marched through – first just the one, then a pair, and within seconds close to a dozen.

Black clad humanoids with opaque helmets to protect their anonymity. Some of them still had snow peppering their shoulders like terrible dandruff. Assault rifles clutched in leather-gloved hands. The red rune emblazoned on the chest plates of their power armour left no doubt they were the Kilonova Corporation's strike force.

They spread out to fill the lobby, their rifles raised, their blank helmets giving no indication the troopers were surprised to discover hundreds of people previously believed to be dead. Karrigan raised his hands to show he wasn't a threat, then tapped the name tag stitched onto his own uniform.

"You're with Kilonova, correct?" he asked. "Name's Karrigan, Head of Security for the *Lucky Quark*. I knew the company would send someone."

One of the troopers emerged from the rest of the group and lifted the visor of their helmet. A craggy, grey face glared at Karrigan from inside, then peered past him at the swarm of residents.

"You're in charge here?"

"As much as anyone is, yes. I've kept order the past few years, brought essential systems online... even made sure the casino's vault remained undisturbed. The ship itself is largely unsalvageable, as I'm sure you're already aware, but—"

The stone-faced squad leader stepped forward and clapped a gloved hand on Karrigan's shoulder.

"And how many of you survived the crash?"

"There are three hundred and sixteen of us left, sir. The rest didn't make it."

The squad leader nodded to one of his anonymous associates and removed his hand from Karrigan's shoulder.

"The official report listed a one hundred percent casualty rate. We're a clean-up crew, you understand, not a rescue team."

"I appreciate that, sir, but we have guests and crew members who need evacuating. It's company policy, not to mention Ministerial law."

The squad leader took another look at all the residents, nodded sagely, and then returned to his silent, unmoving strike force.

"Contingency B, everyone," he barked, sliding his blank visor back down. "Spread out and secure the wreckage."

"Secure the...?" Karrigan snorted and lowered one of his four hands to the gun holster on his hip. "This is a commercial vessel. You talk like you're expecting resistance."

"Just a professional precaution," the squad leader grunted. "Karrigan, was it?"

The *Lucky Quark's* head of security nodded cautiously.

"That'll be all, Karrigan. The company thanks you for your service."

He whipped out a sidearm and shot Karrigan square in the scaly face. The Krolak's body crashed backward through his workstation, knocking over crates and sending paper memos fluttering across the lobby.

The crowd stood in shocked silence for a second. Then the screaming started. People stampeded over one another in their rush to flee the casino. Sheni gasped and ducked down behind the short barrier of his elevated roulette platform while the squad leader holstered his sidearm and checked his rifle.

"Zero survivors," he instructed. "Just like the report says."

CHAPTER NINETEEN

The rattling boom of assault rifles drowned out the screams. Slot machines exploded in showers of sparks and credit chips. Residents dove for cover beneath the card tables and behind the circular planters. Dozens of bodies already littered the entrance to the concourse.

Sheni sprinted across the casino floor, dragging Alan behind him by his spindly arm, until he reached an alcove close to the half-open security door of the food court. Lerrin was crouching behind the decorative pillar beside it.

"What the hell is happening?" Sheni screamed.

"How the stars should I know?" Lerrin yelled in his face. "The company has an obligation to rescue any survivors, not kill them! Do you think a raider gang took out the Kilonova squad and stole their uniforms?"

"I doubt it," Sheni said, risking a peek around the pillar. "I saw the Kilonova frigate in orbit. Not sure when anyone could have wiped out a whole strike force between them landing on-world and driving a small fleet of trucks out here, not without the company noticing."

Mocking clicking sounds to their left. Morton, the insectoid security guard, was hiding with his back pressed against an upturned table.

"Gods, you two are dumb," he said. "Isn't it obvious?"

"What are you doing back here?" Lerrin snapped. "You're part of the security team. You should be up there defending everyone!"

"Are you serious?" Morton flinched as a bullet ricocheted off a nearby glow-lamp. "What good would that do? Have you seen those guys? I wouldn't survive five seconds!"

"What did you mean, isn't it obvious?" Sheni asked, tugging on Alan's arm to keep him from wandering off. "*What's* obvious?"

"The *Lucky Quark* crashed three and a half years ago, right?" Morton tiredly explained. "Well, squatters' rights for any abandoned property within Ministerium controlled space is three years. Not *salvage* rights, scavenger" – this remark was targeted specifically at Sheni – "but rights for the people who actually live there. That means, according to Ministerial law, that everyone still on board the *Lucky Quark* technically has a claim to what's inside that vault. I'm sure Kilonova's lawyers would argue that they've been providing a service to us since the crash, or that the wreckage constitutes an outpost owned and operated by the company, or even that it wasn't *possible* to reclaim it before now, but that's the sort of gobbledegook that gets a case like this stuck in the courts for years. Decades, even. Much cheaper and easier to make sure there are no survivors like their report says."

"Where the hell'd you learn all that?" Sheni asked.

"Law school. I ain't just a hunk of muscle."

"No way," Lerrin said, shaking her head. "Kilonova's a

major corporation. Surely they wouldn't risk wiping out a whole ship just for the sake of a few million credits..."

"Have you seen the kind of investors this casino has?" Morton barked out a short, hysterical laugh. "Of course they would!"

"And everyone thinks you're dead anyway," Sheni muttered. "No-one would ever know."

"Well that's just freakin' great," Lerrin grumbled. "Three years we've waited for rescue, and all this time we'd have been better off left alone. Hell, we'd have been better off if we'd all died in the damn crash."

"Speak for yourself," Morton replied. "I, for one, would quite like to see my family again!"

They all flinched in unison as a stream of rounds peppered the rear wall.

"Doesn't the *Lucky Quark* have any defensive countermeasures?" Sheni asked. "A casino like this was bound to attract raiders sooner or later, you know?"

"Ask Karrigan. Oh wait. You can't!"

"What about the rifles in the Security division? Would they be any good?"

"Better than a handgun," Morton admitted. "Your friend in the holding cells would have brought the weapon cabinets online at the same as the vault access terminal. But you'd still need the passcode and the keys."

"Who has them?"

"Karrigan. So even if you can fish the keys off his belt, good luck unlocking that digi-pad."

"Stars above. Erm, what about the security bots, then? I've seen their booths all over the ship. Aren't they supposed to perform patrols, or something?"

"Sure, and they're designed to take a beating," Lerrin

replied. "Would definitely swing the tide back in our favour. There's just one tiny problem."

"And that is?"

"You can only activate them from the ship's bridge," Morton sighed. "Same issue with the turrets, too."

"Okay." Sheni nodded to Alan, who dribbled. "You two focus on getting everyone to a part of the ship you can lock down tight. Alan and I will head up to the bridge and figure out how to bring its defences online."

"No, that's the problem." Lerrin shook her head. "The bridge is a total mess. It's way too dangerous."

"More dangerous than staying down here?"

Something went *boom* on the floor above. One of the expensive chandeliers suspended over the casino came crashing down in an explosion of broken crystal and neon bulbs.

"I do have one request, though," Sheni shouted over the din. "We need to get Gecki out of that cell."

"Are you kidding?" Morton replied. "She tried to rob us, in case you've forgotten. Deserves everything coming her way."

"So? All things considered, I don't think Kilonova feels like sharing those credits with anyone, do you? Let her out and she can help us!"

Morton grumbled to himself, then tossed his keycard across to Sheni.

"That card will unlock her cell," he said. "Should help get you through any doors on the bridge, in theory, but who knows what state they're in. Best way up there's through Security since the elevator shaft collapsed."

"Thank you. I don't suppose you can give us covering fire while we make a run for it?"

"Fat chance, human," Morton said with another laugh.

"How are we gonna shepherd everyone to safety with those armoured maniacs shooting at us, huh?"

"Yeah, didn't think so. All right, Alan. Stick close, okay?"

"Cyanoacrylate," Alan gurgled agreeably.

Sheni sprinted toward the rear of the casino, darting behind pillars wherever he could. Alan bounced along behind him, his gangly legs barely touching the ground. A bullet whizzed past Sheni's ear close enough for the air to sting. He ducked under the half-open doorframe of the food court and raised a hand to his ear, but it came back clean. Close call.

"You all right, Alan?"

The fluffy ball of Alan's bobble hat was slightly singed, the tussles black and burnt at the ends, but the hat itself was still wrapped firmly over Alan's head. He smiled and babbled incoherently.

They hurried down the food court's promenade. It was mercifully quieter here, and the air smelled of burnt caramel. Something sugary Bena Ursula had left simmering on the stove, Sheni guessed. He wondered if the chef was still breathing. Leaping over a tangled mess of cables stretching across the floor, Sheni raced toward the corridor that connected the food court with the shops on the other side of the ship, then swung himself up the short set of steps. A few manic turns later, and he and Alan were outside the holding cells.

Gecki sat on her bunk, scratching her chin impatiently with her claw. Sheni started to speak, realised she couldn't hear him, and then punched the button on the cell's comm panel.

"What kept you?" she snarled.

"Kilonova's here," he gasped, tapping the keycard

against the panel. "It's, erm, not good. They're wiping out everyone on board the *Quark*."

"*What?* Ah." Comprehension dawned on Gecki's face as she stood up. "Adverse possession, of course. Should have seen that coming. We'd better act quickly, then. Help me get the vault door open. Between the three of us, we can download the credits and have it locked back up before anyone from the company catches on."

"What? No, that's not why I'm freeing you!" Sheni tapped a few buttons and the forcefield in front of Gecki's cell deactivated. "Didn't you hear me? The Kilonova Corporation is slaughtering the remaining survivors. We've got to help them!"

"No, we don't." Gecki emerged from the cell and cracked her neck. "We don't owe these people anything. And it sure doesn't sound like they'll be making much use of these credits any time soon."

"Well, *Gecki*, I'm not hanging about while a bunch of psychotic soldiers hunt everyone down in order to reclaim the exact same fortune *you're* obsessed with!"

"Then if you won't steal the credits," she snarled, "we should take that keycard of yours and drive out of this godsdamn place! If everyone's busy shooting each other, they won't notice us stealing one of their trucks, will they?"

"That's not..." Sheni dug his fingers into his hair and groaned. "You aren't listening to me, Gecki! It's not about getting the credits, or sneaking out before anyone catches us. If the only reason you wanted to drain Kilonova's account was to get rich, that's fine. But be honest about it, you know? Because just half an hour ago you were telling me this whole heist was so you could prove something to your younger self. So you could become the legendary pirate captain you always dreamed of being. Well, stealing a fortune isn't the only way to make a name for yourself, Gecki. You can be notorious for saving people's lives, too."

Gecki grumbled and listened to the distant sound of gunfire.

"Being known as the captain who went claw to claw with the Kilonova Corporation *would* be pretty badass," she mused. "And I bet the survivors wouldn't be too upset if a few credits went missing from the vault afterwards, either..."

"Not exactly the sentiment I was aiming for, but you're on the right track."

"Fine, let's save these pampered idiots." Gecki stomped into the security offices. "Gonna need some guns first."

"Yeah, about that," said Sheni, hurrying after her. "Karrigan had the keys, but he's dead. I don't think we can—"

Gecki punched the old-school padlock hard enough to cut her scaly knuckles open. The padlock shattered and the cabinet door creaked open. The electronic lock didn't even put up a fight.

"Cheap corpo guano," she rasped, scooping out three plasma rifles. "What's the plan, then?"

"Alan and I are gonna head up to the bridge and get the turrets and bots working again. Lerrin said she'd get everyone else someplace safe. You might want to head that way with the guns."

"Gods, *her*? Fine, whatever." She stomped over to the stairwell. "Oh, and Sheni?"

He paused in his efforts to pull an aimless Alan away from the half-eaten churro someone had used to prop up a three legged chair.

"Yeah?"

"Try not to get killed," she rasped, grinning hungrily. "Being rich ain't much fun by myself."

CHAPTER TWENTY

The door to the bridge was located way past the vault, right at the back of Security where the corridors were falling apart. Sheni knew there had once been a better way in and out, an official elevator for the *Quark's* captain and their flight crew, surely, but according to Lerrin and Morton it was in as bad a state as the rest of the ship. It certainly hadn't been featured in the tour.

Gods, he wished he hadn't taken off his enviro-suit. Forget whatever dangers the damaged bridge threw at him. Whole sectors of the ship had been sheered off in the crash. If the bridge was exposed to the elements, he'd quickly freeze to death.

Sheni tapped Morton's keycard against the scanner beside the security door. Nothing happened. No red screen, no bleep of refusal. The power was out, and the door was dead.

He searched for an emergency access panel in case he could unlock the door manually, but if one existed, it had to be on the other side. He hammered his fists on the door, just in case someone had survived in there. Of course nobody answered. Five minutes into his mission and already they were at a dead end. Literally, if the Kilonova goons caught up with them.

"Hey, Alan. Do you reckon you could crawl your way up there, open the door from the other side?"

There was a grate missing from the air vent running overhead. Unlike in the old Earth movies, there was zero chance of Sheni squeezing his way through. But Alan was practically a beach ball with wire brushes for limbs...

Alan stared up at him brainlessly from between his coat and his bobble hat.

"Yeah, course you can. Here, I'll give you a boost."

He lifted Alan up to the missing grate, and Alan enthusiastically scrambled inside. His scrawny legs disappeared into the darkness. Sheni heard the clanging of metal ducts buckling and popping back into shape as his tiny crewmate wriggled down.

"Alan, you still there? Can you hear me?"

Silence. A minute passed. Sheni started to worry. What if Alan had fallen into a gas fire, or impaled himself on a jagged shard of metal? What if the air duct went on for half a mile without an exit? What if—

There was the leaden *thunk* of a lever being pulled, and then the security door rose up on its hydraulic pistons. Alan stood on the other side, smiling blissfully and totally unharmed.

"Nice work, man," Sheni said, beaming. "Next stop... Oh, damn."

Lerrin wasn't kidding when she said the bridge was a mess. No wonder the survivors kept their distance. Chunky rubber cables dangled from the broken ceiling; floor panels were warped or had been flung loose completely; sparks spat from cut wires and water still dripped from busted pipes. The path through the corridor was far from clear, and they hadn't even reached the bridge yet.

"No, we're not going back to Gecki's plan of running away while nobody's looking," he mumbled to Alan. "Don't even think about it."

Alan blinked, one innocent eye slowly swivelling back the way they came.

Sheni crept forwards, hunched low to avoid the cables hanging from the ceiling, arms spread out slightly for balance in case the panels on the floor gave way. Alan dutifully waddled along behind him. Nothing seemed particularly attached to anything anymore. The air was musky and stale, and bitterly cold. Tired metalwork croaked and groaned. He shivered as a globule of coolant dripped onto his neck and trickled down the back of his shirt.

Half of the corridor had collapsed in on itself. Sheni crouched and peered beneath the wreckage. Climbing over wasn't a possibility, and there were no other ways in or out of the bridge. Not without leaving the ship and climbing up the hull, at any rate. The only way through was by crawling underneath.

Alan barged past him, gurgling and giggling to himself, and scurried under the debris.

"Hey, watch yourself!" Sheni hissed, listening to Alan splash about. "There's no knowing how... Oh, who am I kidding? As if we've got any other choice."

He got on his hands and knees and commando-crawled his way under the cave-in. Gods, it was awful. Two inches of gunky water floated above the rusty metal floor. Some parts of the corridor were so tight, Sheni had to hold his breath and dunk half his head under its slimy, filmy surface. It smelled rancid, bad enough that he wanted to breathe only through his mouth, but he didn't dare open it in case he swallowed any of the gunk.

Alan had disappeared. This both worried Sheni and came as nothing of a surprise. He lifted his head to look for him and banged the back of his skull against the iron girder snaking above. Cursing and sucking air through his teeth, he dragged himself through the slippery muck until he found a clump of chalky rubble offering him slightly better grip than the slick metal.

As he pulled at it, the rubble turned. Sheni screamed and let go. It wasn't rubble. It was a Drygg skull stripped of all its chitin and flesh.

Of course. If Lerrin and the other survivors couldn't reach the bridge, they couldn't clear it of dead bodies either. Everyone up here had been left to decompose since the crash.

He scrambled past it, flailing through the water, whacking his knees and elbows against the plastic and aluminium. Soon the collapsed tunnel widened, and he scurried backwards on his hands, panting breathlessly, grateful for the sudden increase in headroom.

Alan watched him from above a pile of ruined computers, inexplicably eating the churro he'd been so desperate to retrieve from the Security division earlier.

"Yeah, thanks for the support, buddy," Sheni said, rising unsteadily to his feet. "Next time, maybe we—"

A loose wire draped through the puddle of water into which he placed his hand. Sheni felt a sharp jolt flash through his body and the next thing he knew, he was lying in a crumpled heap on the far side of the room. His shoulders ached where they'd smashed into the monitor on the wall. His heart beat double-time, as if knocking desperately to be let out of his chest.

Alan appeared at his side and offered him a bite of his churro. Sheni lethargically tore off a relatively un-chewed piece and stuffed it into his numb mouth.

"I'm starting to see why Gecki doesn't like this ship," he mumbled.

His little green companion plucked the keycard from Sheni's pocket and clambered up onto an enormous curved command terminal. Sheni found it difficult to imagine what the bridge had looked like before the disaster. Twice as large as it presently was, no doubt – half of the space was blocked by more collapsed ceilings and buckled bulkheads, and that which he could see was in a tragic state of disrepair. Judging by the scorch marks blackening half the computers, a fire must have broken out following the crash, extinguished either when it ran out of things to burn or when it was doused by the leaking coolant.

Careful not to dip himself into anything electrified again, Sheni pulled himself upright once more and stumbled over to the terminal. He put his hand on the back of a chair for balance. Bad move. It swivelled around on the spot, revealing a skeleton dressed in a dusty *Lucky Quark* uniform.

Sheni was too frazzled to be surprised.

"I guess this guy used to be the captain of the *Quark*. Great job, man. You really nailed it. Xotl never would have got so close to this storm – right, Alan?"

Alan babbled, presumably in agreement, as he continued slapping the keycard against various parts of the command terminal. He must have found something eventually, because the lights and screens and worryingly important-looking flight sticks across its dashboard lit up in bursts and fits.

"Okay, okay..." Sheni tapped the central screen with a

cautious finger. "Let's try not to accidentally activate the ship's thrusters, yeah?"

He scrolled through the ship's directory. Even with his translator implant helping to decipher the alien runes, very little of the operating system made sense to him. It took more than ten minutes to find the listing for turrets and bots, and all the while Sheni's nausea continued to spike. The longer he took getting the defence systems operational, the more innocent people the Kilonova strike force had the opportunity to kill.

"There, I've found it." He tried to switch the features on, but the screen no longer reacted to his touch. "Stars above, why won't it do anything? I'm giving you a command, you stupid machine!"

Alan pottered over and raised a poor corpse's femur above his head like a club.

"Wait," he said, grabbing Alan's hand. "Let me try one more thing before you smash it to smithereens."

Sheni returned to the skeleton on the chair and grimaced as he rummaged through the pockets of its uniform. His fingers closed around a grubby rectangle of plastic.

"Morton's keycard might give him access to every part of the ship," he said, shaking off the grime, "but I bet only people like Karrigan and the captain have the clearance to activate walking weaponry."

He slapped the new card against the scanner built into the terminal. This time when he pressed the touch screen, the icons representing the turrets and security bots turned blue.

"Blue! Blue's good, right? Gods, if those bots start gunning down the guests, Gecki'll never let me hear the end of it."

Sheni backed out of that particular subsystem, but then another folder caught his eye.

"Hey, look at this. The bridge gives me access to all the cameras on the ship, too."

He cycled through the feeds. Many cameras had been shattered in the crash, and plenty more featured nothing but rolling static. He stopped when he found one that showed a stocky, heavily-armed security bot emerge from its unlocked cabinet and stomp past a group of fleeing residents. It didn't so much as twitch a gun barrel at them.

"Thank the stars," he sighed. "Hopefully it's slightly less of a pacifist when it finds the death squad. I suppose it'll give them something else to shoot at, if nothing else."

Sheni went to shut the terminal down, then hesitated. He recognised one of the icons beside the feeds. The camera feature on his data pad had the same one.

"Let's get this on tape," he said, clenching his jaw as he pressed the button. "Kilonova's putting on one hell of a show. It would be a shame for them not to have an audience."

CHAPTER
TWENTY-ONE

Gecki snarled as another ballistic round pinged off the brass trim of a holo-podium and buried itself in the adjacent pillar.

Gods, it would be so easy to slink off and steal everyone's credits. It's not like anyone would miss a million or two. And once you've stolen a couple of million credits, what's the big deal about pinching some evil corporation's rover?

But now it would mean leaving Alan and Sheni behind.

And that's one thing a good captain doesn't do.

She rose from behind the ornate metal wall of her balcony, fired a couple of shots at the pair of Kilonova troopers advancing on her position, and then ducked back into cover before they could reduce her head to a green goo.

"Your crewmates should have reached the bridge by now," Lerrin shouted across to her. "What's taking them so long?"

"Oh, I dunno," she rasped back. "They probably stopped to play a hand of blackjack, or something. Or here's a thought – maybe they're both dead!"

"How can you say that?" Lerrin looked genuinely appalled. "They're your friends!"

"The regard I hold for my fellow crew members has little bearing on their odds of survival." Gecki rolled her one good eye. "Now quit yapping and make use of the guns I brought you!"

Once Sheni had freed Gecki from her cell, she'd sprinted towards the casino floor with a bundle of rifles clutched to her chest. A few distraught residents had flocked the other direction, as had one of the security officers she'd seen flanking Karrigan back when she was first brought to the reception lobby. Then she'd stumbled across the first of many bodies perforated by the strike force, witnessed another wall of one-armed bandits topple over in a cascade of gears, glass and shiny plastic.

"Where's that Lerrin girl?" she'd snarled as she grabbed the squishy arm of somebody fleeing past.

"I saw her leading people towards the observation deck," the semi-gelatinous cephalopod spluttered. "But that's where most of those armed lunatics are headed, too!"

"Same goes for me, I guess," she grumbled to herself, stomping off in the described direction.

There was no use in approaching the observation deck from the front. Not unless she fancied switching allegiances – maybe in exchange for her services, Kilonova would hand over a sackful of cash rather than put a bullet in her head. Unlikely. Besides, if Lerrin had any sense the place would be locked down tighter than their godsdamn vault. But there were always back-door maintenance corridors, and Gecki still had a vague recollection of how to reach them from when she skimmed over the *Quark's* schematics prior to landing on Gressil Prime.

She stalked across to the commercial promenade full of

defunct shops, then instead of taking a left back towards the Security division, she went right. A slim doorway was nestled in the corner, barely distinguishable from the rest of the digital billboards covering the dented walls. The electronic lock was busted. She pried the door open with a claw and slipped inside.

The narrow stairwell was dark, derelict, and had clearly been left forgotten for the past three years. Motes of dust lingered motionlessly like the ice crystals of Saturn's rings. Cobwebs and cocoons of dead bugs littered the ceiling. But the hallway at the top of the steps wasn't deserted. Gecki heard hushed whispers as she reached the summit. Quietly depositing the rifles on the ground, she adjusted the colour of her scales to match her gloomy surroundings.

Two Kilonova-branded troopers were attempting to break through a door. One was crouching with a plasma torch primed to cut through its bolts. The other leaned against the wall beside him, arms crossed.

"This ain't exactly what I agreed to," the trooper with the crossed arms grunted. "Was just meant to be a simple cash extraction."

"So what?" replied the other. "You've done ops like this before, ain't ya? Get paid the same either way."

"Yeah, sure. But it's nice to know how much—"

Gecki slashed a claw under the helmet of the trooper leaning against the wall. Blood spurted out from his neck in a sudden torrent, splashing the shoulders of his colleague crouched below. By the time the other squad member had stood up and spun around in shock, Gecki had already spilled half his intestines on the floor.

Grimacing as her bare feet splashed against the spreading pool of blood, she banged her fist on the locked door.

"Oi, Lerrin. You in there? It's Gecki. You know, the dirty thief you guys locked up."

The door hissed open. Morton was on the other side with his gun pointed at Gecki's face. The barrel was shaking wildly. Lerrin stood close behind. Gecki smiled with too much teeth.

"Sheni said you might need these," she said, scooping up the guns.

"About time," Lerrin replied, taking one rifle and shoving another into Morton's insectoid hands. "We barricaded everyone we could find inside the viewing gallery, but it won't be long until Kilonova's brutes break through."

Gecki peered through the slitted windows in the armoured barrier to her left. Over a hundred residents and former crew members huddled amongst the rows of torn seats. The grand observation windows were shielded from the storm outside by reinforced shutters. To her right was a set of mirrored staircases, at the bottom of which was another hefty security door. She could hear locks being sheared through with lasers on the other side.

"Then we'd best make sure that's the only door they open," Gecki snarled, taking up position behind the balcony wall.

And so they'd waited. When the exterior set of doors finally grunted apart, Gecki popped the first trooper she saw in the helmet with a round from her rifle. A barrage of ballistics had streamed their way in immediate retaliation. They'd been pretty much pinned down since.

"Get a move on, Sheni," she muttered as Lerrin took a turn shooting at the half a dozen intruders slowly pressing forward into the lobby of the observation deck. "Fighting for a good cause is all well and good, but I'm sure not dying for one…"

A curved cabinet concealed within the wooden panels of the stern-facing wall slid open. A stocky robot shaped like a pointy-headed filing cabinet barged out on a pair of short, rubbery legs.

"Cease fire," Morton shouted, spinning around to face Gecki and Lerrin. "Don't give the bot any reason to—"

A round from one of the troopers clipped Morton on the shoulder. He crashed to the floor, luminous green gunk seeping from the hole in his uniform. Lerrin darted across and pulled him back to safety behind the balcony's barrier.

The security bot, detecting the violence, turned and stomped down the curved stairwell toward the Kilonova strike force. Alarmed, the squad ceased firing on the balcony and instead targeted the new intruder. Plenty of rounds dented, even punctured the bot's chassis, but the cold, expressionless bot was relentless. It kept advancing even as the LED bulbs on its front shattered and popped.

Then the six barrels on the underside of its left arm began to spin, blurring as a shrill whir filled the hall.

A wide spray of bullets tore across the squad like a power-wash. Half of the troopers were fortunate enough to reach cover in time. The others were annihilated in a cloud of rubble, brass shrapnel and blood. Body parts splattered against the marble floor amidst a patter of scarlet rain.

Gecki peered over the top of the balcony. Her lips peeled back in a triumphant grin as a pungent iron stench filled her nostrils.

Now *this* was more like it.

The surviving goons made a run for it back the way they came, back toward the rattling din of more security bots defending the ship's guests. The observation deck's own robo-guard lowered its rotary cannon, switched to the semi-automatic precision rifle on the underside of its right arm, and shot one of the fleeing marines clean through the back.

Heavy clanging footsteps as somebody raced up toward them through the side tunnel. Gecki spun around with her rifle raised.

"Watch where you point that thing," Sheni gasped, throwing his hands in the air as he burst into the lobby. Alan waddled out from behind him. The tiny guy was carrying an old bone.

Morton let out a groan. Gecki gave him a withering look. The wound wasn't *that* bad. A splash of antiseptic and a sling and the dumb insect would be back eating fancy Bursaagu pastries in no time.

She plucked up Morton's discarded rifle and passed it to Sheni.

"We've got to keep moving," he said, hands on his knees, out of breath. "The bots and turrets are pushing the strike force back towards the shuttle bay!"

"You two go," Lerrin said. "I'll stay here with Morton and keep watch in case any more corporate nut jobs show up."

Gecki and Sheni hurried out of the observation deck's lobby, their heads low, ducking behind whatever cover the connecting corridor offered them. Alan happily tottered along behind like a kid being taken to the circus. What remained of the Kilonova squad was long gone, but they anxiously passed the security bot still waddling along in slow pursuit. Despite the rifles in their arms, it didn't so much as bleep at them in warning.

Emerging onto the casino floor, they flinched in unison as a thunderous boom rang out through the enormous chamber. A gunmetal grey twin-cannoned sentry turret – the sort Gecki usually expected to find on the *outside* of ships – had descended from one of the finely sculpted circles in the casino's ceiling and was methodically blasting troopers apart before they could escape through the doors to the shuttle bay.

"You know what?" Sheni said, shrugging as he deposited his rifle onto the nearest card table. "I don't think it's worth the risk."

Only three members of the strike force remained. The craggy-faced leader who shot Karrigan threw down his rifle and raised his hands above his head. The two other troopers quickly did the same. The turret swivelled to face them but held fire. As did the half a dozen security bots still making their plodding journey toward them from various sectors of the ship.

Sheni and Gecki dodged the occasional corpse and bloody smear as they jogged across the casino floor to the reception lobby, where the last three marines had already dropped to their knees with their hands clasped behind their helmets. Seven or eight residents not holed up in the observation deck crept out from hiding places to join them. A particularly tearful guest kicked one trooper repeatedly in the small of his back, and had to be forcibly dragged away by their neighbour.

"I expect *you* don't want to kill them." Gecki snorted to Sheni as she eyed the survivors. "Good luck convincing this lot, softie."

"Then let's move them quickly," Sheni replied. "You know exactly where they ought to go."

CHAPTER
TWENTY-TWO

With the three surviving members of the strike force incarcerated in the Security division – one trooper for each of the three forcefield-protected cells – Sheni and Gecki returned to the reception lobby where the remaining residents of the *Lucky Quark* had convened. Both were back in their enviro-suits. Bena Ursula was present. So was the elderly Luethian who'd reattached Alan's button. The dead-eyed octopod Sheni had seen playing on the one-armed bandit machines was gone.

Some of the bodies were still being carried out of the casino hall. Families gathered around those they'd lost, crying and mourning. Little could be done about the blood dripping from the card tables, the pillars and the slot machines at that present moment. A couple of security officers stood guard by the corridor leading down to the shuttle bay, accompanied by a small fireteam of dutiful sentry bots, just in case a second wave of Kilonova goons decided to show up.

Lerrin seemed to have taken over as de facto leader in

Karrigan's stead, standing beside his upturned workstation where his body had recently lain until others had carried it reverently into the snow outside. He would be buried along with all the others, in so much as anything can be buried in soil as hard as rock, once essential repairs were made and life support systems were confirmed to still be operational. The bodies would keep in the cold. Morton stood beside her, forever the second-in-command, his wound bandaged and his affected arm cradled in a makeshift sling.

Sheni handed Morton his security keycard.

"You'll be needing this back," he said. "Those murderers aren't going anywhere. Up to you what you do with them once we're gone, I guess."

"I'll make sure no harm comes to them," Morton replied. "Nothing serious, anyway. They're our new bargaining chip."

"Aren't all the credits on board this ship enough?" Gecki scoffed.

"Oh, Kilonova's not getting their hands on any of that," Lerrin replied, crossing her arms. "Not a single damn credit. I reckon it's owed to the people here who've lost everything, don't you?"

"Finders keepers," Gecki rasped with no small amount of irritation.

"Not sure that's the exact phrase the Ministerium uses," Sheni said, smirking, "but close enough. You're taking quite the gamble, you know, banking on Kilonova to care about a few grunts. And credits aren't worth much if you can't spend them. Do you really think this ship's gonna hold itself together another fifteen years?"

Worried muttering swept through the gathered crowd. Most of the survivors would have resigned themselves to a life on board the *Quark* after the crash. But Sheni and

Gecki's arrival, and then that of the Kilonova strike force so soon afterwards... it had sown hope of rescue where the soil ought to have been barren. Clearly a number of residents had forgotten that their palace was crumbling down around their ears.

"I refuse to believe there's no technology out there that'll get Kilonova through this storm." Lerrin shook her head. "Them, or some other organisation. Look what the Mansa Empire can do with solar cores. You're telling me *they'd* be put off by some strong winds?"

"Of course not," Gecki rasped. "But the Mansa Empire, Kilonova ain't. If Kilonova had the tech, could even *afford* the tech, they'd have come got the *Quark* long before now."

"So we force their hand," Lerrin replied, loudly so everyone could hear. "They won't come for us, or their captured grunts. They won't even come for their credits, not if it's gonna cost them more to get here than they can possibly recoup from their vault. But they'll have to fork out if the alternative is a galaxy-wide PR disaster, even if it brings them close to bankruptcy. Sheni. I'm guessing you were the one who got all the cameras rolling, right?"

Sheni nodded. "Got them backed up, anyway."

Lerrin retrieved a data drive from Karrigan's computer setup and pressed it into his palm.

"Here. I ripped all the video from the intact feeds. It shows Karrigan's murder, the slaughter of innocent Quark residents and employees, the whole lot. Get out of this storm and then send the footage to every news station on the extranet. Will you do that for us?"

"Yeah, of course," Sheni said, pocketing the drive. "Least we can do, you know?"

"Well, not the *least* you could do," Gecki snarled.

"Gecki..."

"Is something the matter?" Lerrin asked, the question pointed more towards Sheni than his cantankerous reptilian companion.

"She's just cranky because we didn't make off with millions from your vault," Sheni sighed. "That's the only reason we came out here. We've got this dodgy Felisian art collector on our backs, you see, and she says she'll hunt us down and kill us if we don't fork over two hundred thousand credits..."

"What?" Lerrin's eyes grew massive. "Are you kidding? That's insane! How in the galaxy did you end up in such a stupid position?"

"Broke a window," Sheni muttered.

"Stars above." Lerrin waved Morton over. "Fetch what they need from the vault, okay? Two hundred thousand credits is just a drop in the ocean as far as those reserves are concerned, but if it'll keep our new friends from getting eviscerated, what the hell."

They waited patiently, and slightly awkwardly, while Morton marched off in the direction of the Security offices. The crowd continued to gossip excitedly at the prospect of an actual rescue.

"You could have told her we owe Patheer three hundred thousand," Gecki whispered. "Give us *some* spending money, at least."

"Just be grateful your scaly hide won't be turned into Patheer's new scratching post any time soon," Sheni muttered back.

Morton returned five minutes later and shoved one of the vault's small black lockboxes into Sheni's arms.

"Two hundred thousand credits," he said begrudgingly. "You can count them if you want."

"Thank you," Sheni said, sincerely, before repeating

himself more loudly for the sake of everybody else watching. "Thank you. This means the world to us, doesn't it, Gecki?"

Gecki generated a guttural growl from deep in her throat, but she managed to force a sharp-toothed smile.

"Someone will come soon," Sheni said to Lerrin in what he hoped was a reassuring tone. "A real extraction team, next time. The Ministry will send someone if they have to, right? We'll make sure everyone knows what happened here today. Kilonova won't get away with this."

"Of course they will. They can deny their involvement, say the strike force wasn't operating under their orders. But either way, they'll have to pull out all the stops once the galaxy realises we aren't dead. Well. Those of us who are left, obviously."

They looked out at the *Lucky Quark's* dwindling population. Even Gecki winced, though admittedly it didn't look much different to her sneer.

"Yeah, well, on that cheery note. Shall we?"

They gave everyone a half-hearted wave goodbye, which went unnoticed by most of the survivors, and descended the corridor leading down to the shuttle bay, where hopefully they'd find a new set of wheels. Sheni spoke quietly so his voice wouldn't carry.

"What are we gonna do if the Kilonova Corporation's rovers are fitted with biometric locks?"

"Rip the arm off a grunt's corpse," Gecki replied, shrugging. "What are you looking at me like that for? You want to get back to the *Silver Hart*, don't you? Where there's a will, Sheni, there's a way."

CHAPTER
TWENTY-THREE

Sheni trudged through the deep snow with his head lowered against the wind and the lockbox clutched against his chest. Maybe it was just his imagination, but he didn't remember the eye of the storm being this harsh before. If the brief lull was coming to an end, they needed to get back to Borel-Six pronto.

"That rover," Gecki rasped over comms, tapping Sheni on the shoulder of his enviro-suit.

"Why that one?" Sheni shouted back. There were others slightly closer.

"Looks the biggest," she insisted. "I'm not taking any chances."

Sheni scrutinised the other black and red vehicles as he plodded towards Gecki's pick. What if the strike force had stationed getaway drivers inside the vehicles? Sheni and Gecki had left their rifles behind on the Lucky Quark. The snow kept them from moving quickly. There'd be no running to cover, no closing the distance and taking them out hand-to-hand. If any Kilonova troops remained, he and Gecki would be shot in seconds.

He spotted the rover they'd leased from Drairy and winced. It was in an even worse state than he remembered. Half of the panels were missing from its skeletal frame, the rear wheels were twisted askew, and the storm had filled its corpse with snow. His gut told him Drairy didn't have insurance for this sort of thing...

They stalked up to the chunky, armoured rover and sidled along its flank. Its tank treads were almost as tall as Sheni. He stood on tip toes, peeked through the window of the driver's side door, and relaxed. The vehicle was empty. And when he tried the door, it opened freely.

They both tried to climb up into the driver's seat.

"Are you kidding?" Sheni hissed. "You think I'm gonna let you take the wheel after what you did to our last ride?"

"Fine," Gecki grumbled as she skulked around to the passenger side. "Just don't try taking any shortcuts this time, you hear me?"

They climbed in and slammed the doors shut behind them. Even with Sheni's enviro-suit having kept the worst of the chill at bay, the interior of the rover was significantly warmer. He removed his helmet and took a big gulp of climate-controlled air.

"Do you think anyone on board the *Quark* will drive the other rovers out of here?" he asked.

"Maybe one or two will chance it, but probably not. Ain't enough wheels for everyone. Some people would be left behind. Wouldn't be fair, would it?"

"Same reason no-one begged to come with us when they had the opportunity, I guess. Not that the *Quark's* all that bad a place to be holed up a little while longer. I can see why some would stay."

"That, and they don't have a clue where to go. Speaking of which – get this rover moving, won't you?"

Sheni hesitated. He counted himself, Gecki, the lockbox nestled between their seats...

"Aren't we missing something?"

Their eyes grew wide with appalled realisation.

"Alan!" they said in unison.

Doors slammed shut at the rear of the cabin. By the time they twisted around, Alan was already strapped into one of the seats lining the rover's flank and chewing contently on a fresh churro. The blizzard had transformed the bobble of his woolly hat into a snowball.

"Transitory sustenance," he gurgled, one eye performing a full three hundred and sixty degree loop.

"Whatever you say, man," Sheni sighed. "Now, let's see if we can even switch this beast on..."

He scoured the dashboard in search of an On button. After a few seconds, Gecki reached across and flicked a switch an inch below the steering levers. The rover quivered as its engine roared.

"I would have found it," Sheni muttered under his breath.

"Eventually," Gecki replied loudly.

Sheni inputted the coordinates for Borel-Six into the rover's NavMap. The satellite guidance system was still haywire due to the storm, but at least it told him which way was west. That was a start.

"Here goes nothing," he said, slowly edging the rover forward. "Second time's the charm, right?"

Their rover climbed the rocky banks and disappeared into the swirling snow.

"Hang a left," Gecki growled.

"What do you think I'm trying to do?" Sheni replied, wrenching the control levers as far toward port as they'd go.

"Hang a left, godsdammit!"

The rover bulldozed through an archway of blue ice. Chunks the size of watermelons crashed over its windscreen. Gecki threw back her head and hissed.

"Gah! Not even Kilonova tech is built to withstand hits like that, Sheni!"

For almost two hours they'd been driving, and the storm hadn't let up once. First they'd braved the tornadoes, including more of the flaming variety, and lightning bolts fierce enough to melt steel and aluminium. Then came the dense blizzards that left them blind, forcing them to roll through the tundra at a crawl. And now, even as they surely reached the storm's furthest snow band, the hurricane winds threatened to at best overturn them, at worst toss them off yet another cliff.

The tank treads lost what little grip they possessed. The rover skidded sideways, almost flipped onto its back, but then righted itself at the last second. Alan bounced up and down in his seat. Sheni glanced at the NavMap. They were facing almost the completely wrong direction.

"Stars, you're hopeless," Gecki snapped. "Look how close we are, yet you keep pulling right. Why are you pulling right?"

"Go on, then – *you* give that lever a tug! See what difference it makes!"

The drivetrain croaked as Sheni struggled to point the vehicle west again. For all its fancy stabilisers and thick armour, the Kilonova Corp's truck was struggling. Even if

Drairy's rover had made the initial trip intact, it never would have survived this.

"Don't conk out on me now," Sheni grunted through gritted teeth. "Just a little bit more…"

Drairy was halfway through piecing the dented wing of a delivery shuttle back together when she heard a strange noise outside her garage.

The mournful moan of a whale who's lost a calf, it sounded like, followed by the unmistakable clang of metal on metal.

"Probably those dumb off-worlders with my rover," she grunted to herself, cleaning the grease off her leathery hands with a rag. "Least they're early, I s'pose."

Drairy tossed the rag to one side, threw on a thick woolly coat over her stained overalls, and left her workshop for the frostbitten garage. She punched the button to open the exterior doors in the control booth before returning to the chamber with her hands tucked in her pockets. She shivered from head to elephantine toe. Even for an Alpha Rhoden, the weather outside was freakin' chilly.

Wispy spectres floated up past her horn from her hooded nostrils. The parade of apparitions suddenly stopped as her breath caught in her throat. She was far too surprised to be cold anymore.

This wasn't her rover. It was worth substantially more credits than her rover, sure, but that wasn't the point. This tank would barely fit inside her garage. That said, if she fixed up those axles and differentials, and if she sand-blasted the Kilonova logo off its side…

She checked the cabin. It was empty. Any footprints in

the snow had already been brushed away by the wind. Drairy looked both ways through the deserted tundra, then back at the abandoned rover.

"Gods," she said, hands on hips. "What am I s'posed to do with this?"

Sheni and Gecki collapsed inside the *Silver Hart's* airlock, remaining slumped against its walls long after the decontamination cycle was complete. Alan pottered past them, hung up his coat and hat in the same closet Sheni and Gecki's enviro-suits were destined for, and then waddled off in the direction of the engine room.

Quite unusually for their starfish pilot, Xotl hadn't descended the steps to greet them. Sheni called out to them as he climbed up to the cockpit.

"Get the ship's comm system ready," he said, out of breath. "We've got a lot of messages to send out."

"Yes, well, that's fine," Xotl replied impatiently. "But do you mind if we do it from orbit? I fear the ship won't hold together if we remain on this horrid rock much longer."

Sheni sagged into his seat at the rear of the cockpit and listened to the soft groaning of the fuselage. The wind here was barely strong enough to strip paint, let alone pull off a thruster. He couldn't help but laugh.

"You have no idea what we've been through, you know?"

"Evidently. I've been stuck here alone – for much longer than you estimated, might I add – worrying that the three of you were dead. I don't suppose we're millionaires yet?"

"Of course not," Gecki snarled irately as she joined them. "But we might be debt free."

"That'll be a first," Xotl spluttered, raising the ship from its landing pad.

The *Silver Hart* shuddered as she climbed through the fierce clouds, and Sheni was quickly reminded of why Xotl was so apprehensive. The bolts rattled. The ship jerked to the left and right as it fought Xotl's commands. The NavMap was supposed to guide them around the worst of the storm clouds, but it amended itself with such frequency it was practically impossible to follow.

The purple starfish was far more attuned to the ship's wellbeing than either him or Gecki. Maybe a day spent exposed to the elements had done more damage to their ride than Sheni wanted to believe...

He gripped the arms of his chair hard, closed his eyes, and fought to shut out the memory of their rover being ripped apart, panel by panel...

And then it was over. He opened his eyes and saw stars instead of storm clouds. The *Silver Hart* floated effortlessly through the void like a drunk sunbather on an inflatable lilo.

"Please tell me we will never be visiting Gressil Prime again," Xotl spluttered, spinning around in their egg-seat. "Unless you plan on using some of those credits to buy us a flying tank."

"With the amount we're gonna be left with, we'll be lucky to afford a tankard of beer." Sheni rose from his seat and plugged the data drive Lerrin gave him into the dashboard. "Now, about that comm system, Xotl?"

Sheni compiled a list of every major Kapamentis news channel he could think of while Xotl pulled up a list of corresponding comm IDs. If they reported on the massacre on board the *Lucky Quark*, the thousands of smaller networks in the outer systems would soon follow.

"And... sent." Sheni leaned against Gecki's terminal. "No guarantee that anybody will actually open a file sent to them from some random spacer, but we only need one reporter to watch that video, you know?"

"We've done all we can to help those people," Gecki rasped. She shook the lockbox. "What are we going to do about *this?*"

Sheni weighed their options. Two hundred thousand credits. It was damn tempting to run off with it, but they'd have a target on their backs for the rest of their lives. It would be a damn fun week, though.

But if they returned to Patheer's penthouse, who was to say the bloodthirsty crook wouldn't take the money and then kill them anyway?

An idea came to him.

"Patheer likes a hunt, right?" Sheni composed one final message. "Well, if she wants two hundred thousand credits in exchange for our lives, the least she can do is come to us."

CHAPTER
TWENTY-FOUR

Somebody slammed a card onto a rickety wooden table hard enough to knock dust out of the grain, chortled in triumph, and then scooped the pile of credits in the middle of the table toward them with a big, hairy arm. Somebody growled and plunged a knife into the table. Then the table got overturned, cards, knife and all.

Copper John rose from behind the bar and levelled a shotgun at the gamblers.

"If you can't play nice," the cranky automata said in his electronic voice, "I'll make sure you don't play at all. Scudd, you want to buy your friends there a round with those winnings, huh?"

Scudd, a heavy-browed ogreish creature, grumbled in the affirmative as he righted the table. His opponents cheered and slapped the giant on the shoulder. Everyone else crowding inside the Corpse & Casket went back to their rowdy conversations.

Sheni turned back to Gecki and shrugged. So long as his drink didn't get knocked over, he wasn't too fussed what went on in the rest of the bar. They still hadn't paid off their increasingly hefty bar tab, and he highly doubted Copper John would stretch it much further.

"I've gotta say," Gecki rasped between conservative sips of beer, "this is one of the better ideas you've had. The Corpse & Casket's the ideal spot for a handover. It's somehow quiet and busy at the same time."

"Thanks, I guess. It's just a precaution. I figure deep down Patheer cares more about making credits than she does chasing us across the galaxy, you know?"

"I dunno, Sheni." Gecki shifted uneasily in her seat. "Felisians can sure hold a grudge. But for once their superiority complex might work in our favour. Give it a few more days and maybe she'll have forgotten all about us..."

"Well, if Patheer decides not to honour our agreement," Sheni said, exhaling deeply, "she'll find plenty of people here eager for a fight."

Alan, who was sitting between the two of them, gurgled innocently.

"Heads up," Gecki snarled, her lips peeling back from her teeth. "We've got company."

A Felisian in fitted body armour walked through the doorway of the Corpse & Casket, a revolted expression stamped on his face. He sneered at the drunken Oortilian stumbling past him. Sheni recognised the big cat from Patheer's penthouse – he was the white and grey haired bodyguard who'd left halfway through their interrogation. Clearly Patheer didn't stoop so low as to attend her own drop-offs. The bodyguard spotted Sheni and Gecki in the centre of the bar and stalked across to their table with his chest puffed out.

"Pull up a stool," Gecki snarled with a swish of her claws.

"I'd rather stand," the Felisian purred, glancing down at the reptilian with disdain. "Do you have the credits?"

"One hundred thousand, wasn't it?" Sheni asked, trying his luck one last time.

"Each," the bodyguard growled impatiently. "Don't waste my time, human. Do you have them or not?"

Three inch claws extended from the Felis Vestris's huge hands.

"Woah, man, we've got it." Sheni hurriedly slid the black lockbox across the table. "It's all there, all right? Every last credit."

Patheer's bodyguard didn't take his word for it. He snatched up the lockbox and slowly probed through its contents. Sheni and Gecki waited in silence. Alan slurped a fruit juice through a straw.

"Very well," he finally said, slamming the lockbox shut. "In accordance with the Prowler's Rite, consider the hunt lifted and your debt cleared. But if Patheer ever sees you skulking around her district again..."

"She'll slit our throats and sink us to the bottom of the Tonsha Waterway," Sheni replied, swallowing hard. "Yeah, don't worry. We'll stay out of Patheer's fur."

The bodyguard grinned.

"It's funny," he said, carving a claw through the table to inspect the dirt. "Patheer very nearly sent you to break into that *Lucky Quark* ship, if you can believe it. She lost a lot of credits when that casino went down, what with being an investor and all. But we know how *that* turned out, don't we? Bloodbath's all over the extranet. You'd both be dead by Kilonova's hand rather than Patheer's, *and* she'd be none the richer."

"Wow, yeah," Sheni said, sharing a nervous glance with

Gecki. "Good thing she put a mark on our heads instead, right?"

"Indeed. You know, Patheer really didn't think you'd make good on this. Had the hunting craft stocked and prepped for launch. But the rules of the Rite must be honoured. Just remember, scum. Next time she catches you, you won't get a chance to run."

The bulky Felisian turned from their table with a flourish and marched out of the bar. Sheni and Gecki visibly sagged with relief the moment he disappeared through the doorway.

"Did we just pay Patheer back with her own money?" Sheni whispered urgently.

"Gods, now I *really* wish we'd taken more of it..."

One of the Krolaks towards the rear of the bar fell backward off their chair. A drunk Drygg broke into a shanty, which usually only stopped once the whole bar finished the song together or someone put a knife through the culprit's throat. Fortunately for the Drygg, this time it was the former. Voices were raised. Much beer was sloshed.

Gecki stared around at the boisterous bar and sighed.

"Round and round in circles. Same damn place."

Sheni winked and elbowed her in the ribs.

"Cheer up, Gecki. The next take's gonna be the big one. I can feel it."

"All I can feel is a headache coming on," she snarled, scratching her snout.

Alan slipped off his chair and waddled through the merry pirate captains to the bar. He clambered up onto the stool beside a semi-conscious Old Guntho, whose head kept dipping against the bartop. Copper John eyed the green jelly bean curiously with his telescopic lens.

"Not you again. What d'you want?"

Alan slammed a bunch of credits from the *Lucky Quark's* vault on the counter.

"Panoramic inebriation," he gurgled.

"I have no idea what that means," Copper John replied. "Bolts alive, son. There's over four hundred credits here."

"I think," Old Guntho groaned through sluggish lips, "he wants to buy us all a drink."

"You can understand him?" Copper John asked. "That true, little fellow? You want to buy everyone here a round? Or three," he added, poking through the credits with a metal digit.

One of Alan's eyes gradually rotated to stare at the pint clasped in Old Guntho's wrinkly fist. Then he stuck out his arms rigidly to either side, so he was standing on his stool like a scarecrow.

"I'll take that as a yes," the old automata said, brushing the credits into his coin receptacle. "You're about to be very popular round these parts, son."

Alan continued smiling at the rows of liquor lined up behind the bar like he hadn't heard a word the automata said.

Copper John clunked and wheezed his way down to the far end of the bar and pressed a button screwed into a wooden beam. A deep klaxon tore through the drinking hall. Everybody in the Corpse & Casket cheered, Sheni and Gecki included. Mugs overflowing with ale were hastily pressed into greedy hands and tentacles. Shanties were resumed with vastly increased vigour and volume.

Alan observed all of this with a face as slow as a glacier and a mind as fast as a... well, perhaps not a particle accelerator, but at least a bubbling brook in which an idea was brewing.

Sheni had been right when he said their next big take was just around the corner.

They just needed some help figuring out which corner it was.

THANK YOU FOR READING!

The adventure continues in Shadows in the Stone.

And you might want to check out The Final Dawn if you haven't already – it's the series in which Sheni and the crew of the *Silver Hart* first make an appearance.

Turn the page for a full list of titles set in the same universe as Shadows in the Snow.

BOOKS IN THE "DARK STAR PANORAMA" UNIVERSE

Final Dawn Series

- The Final Dawn
- Thief of Stars
- A Dark Horizon
- The New World
- The Tin Soldiers
- Ghost of the Father
- The Stellar Abyss
- The Edge of Night
- The Fatal Dark

War for New Terra Series

- Sigma
- Iron Nest
- Royal Blood

Shadows in the Stars Series

- Shadows in the Stars
- Shadows in the Snow
- Shadows in the Stone

Kapamentis Crime Series

- A Cut Below
- Cut to the Bone
- Cut and Shut

- The Final Cut

Standalone Novels

- Saturnalia

SELECT NON-DSP TITLES

- Checking Out (Box Set)
- Blackwater (Box Set)
- The Portrait Lingers Like a Whisper
- Gerald Oddman

WANT A FREE, EXCLUSIVE BOOK?

Building a relationship with my readers is one of the best things about writing. Every now and then I send out newsletters with details on new releases, special offers and other bits of news relating to my books.

And if you sign up to the mailing list I'll even send you a **FREE** copy of *The Ultimate Dark Star Panorama Compendium*, an exclusive guide covering every aspect of my Dark Star Panorama universe, from a full timeline to a comprehensive encyclopaedia. It also contains *Before the Dawn*, a short prequel to my *Final Dawn* series.

Sign up today at twmashford.com.

ENJOY THIS BOOK? YOU CAN MAKE A BIG DIFFERENCE.

Reviews are the most powerful tool in my arsenal when it comes to getting attention for my books. As an indie author, I don't have quite the same financial muscle as a New York publisher. But what I *do* have is something even more effective:

A committed and loyal bunch of readers.

Honest reviews of my books help bring them to the attention of other readers.

If you've enjoyed this book I would be very grateful if you could spend just five minutes leaving a review (it can be as short as you like) on the book's Amazon page.

Thank you very much.

ABOUT THE AUTHOR

Tom Ashford lives just outside London, England with his wife Jenny and extremely needy cat, Kathleen.

An avid movie buff and video game addict, Tom loves all things science fiction. That's why he started the *Dark Star Panorama* universe – an ever-growing tapestry of epic spacefaring stories including the *Final Dawn, Kapamentis Crime* and *War for New Terra* series.

His favourite authors are Terry Pratchett and Stephen King.

facebook.com/TWMAshford

instagram.com/ashfordtom

Printed in Great Britain
by Amazon